Myths Beyond Dragons

Dragon Shifter Romance

Mac Flynn

All names, places, and events depicted in this book are fictional and products of the author's imagination.

No part of this publication may be reproduced, stored in a retrieval system, converted to another format, or transmitted in any form without explicit, written permission from the publisher of this work. For information regarding redistribution or to contact the author, write to the publisher at the following address.

Crescent Moon Studios, Inc.
P.O. Box 117
Riverside, WA 98849

Website: www.macflynn.com
Email: mac@macflynn.com

ISBN / EAN-13: 9781791814441

Copyright © 2018 by Mac Flynn

First Edition

CONTENTS

Chapter 1..1
Chapter 2..7
Chapter 3..13
Chapter 4..20
Chapter 5..30
Chapter 6..35
Chapter 7..42
Chapter 8..50
Chapter 9..55
Chapter 10..61
Chapter 11..65
Chapter 12..72
Chapter 13..80
Chapter 14..87
Chapter 15..93
Chapter 16..99
Chapter 17..108
Chapter 18..114
Chapter 19..121
Chapter 20..127
Chapter 21..133
Chapter 22..138

Chapter 23..146
Chapter 24..154
Chapter 25..160
Chapter 26..165
Chapter 27..171
Chapter 28..176
Chapter 29..182
Chapter 30..190
Chapter 31..198
Chapter 32..205
Chapter 33..213
Chapter 34..220
Chapter 35..227
Chapter 36..234

Continue the adventure.................................242
Other series by Mac Flynn...........................247

MYTHS BEYOND DRAGONS

CHAPTER 1

They just wouldn't stop popping up. Like those dots you see when you look at the sun too long, no matter how hard I tried to look away the visions were still there.

That's why I stood at the edge of the lake in Alexandria. The shoreline was touched by ice, but three yards into the lake the water lay open. The shadows didn't touch me here, or so I hoped. Behind me towered the ancient water temple, and between us stood the arch that guided the path up to the religious building.

I raised my hand and studied the palm. The tips of my fingers were a little red, but the unmistakable color of my skin gave me comfort.

A cool breeze blew past me and across the late, disturbing the tranquil scene for a brief moment. I wrapped my coat tighter around myself and shivered. "You'd think a water fae wouldn't get cold. . ." I muttered.

"Temperature and water are very different," a voice spoke up. I spun around and found Xander walking down the path toward me with a teasing smile on his face.

My own face fell as he came up beside me. "How'd you know I was here?"

He nodded at my covered shoulder. "I always know where you are."

I pressed my hand on the part of my coat that lay over the mark and looked out over the lake. The water was as calm as glass, and just as reflective. The castle across the lake was illuminated with candles, and a perfect picture of it lay on the watery surface.

"Something troubles you," Xander spoke up.

I snorted. "Does my mark tell you that, too?"

He gently cupped my chin in his hand and turned my face so we gazed into each other's eyes. His were penetrating. "I do not need help to know when you are bothered, I need only your help to tell me what it is that bothers you."

I bit my lower lip and cast my eyes to the ground. "I'm not really sure myself, and it's really hard to explain."

"I will try to understand," he replied.

My eyes flickered up to his face and I frowned at him. "This isn't funny. I really think there's something wrong with me."

His eyebrows crashed down and all humor fled his face. "You are ill?"

I shook my head. Then I shrugged. "I don't know." A snort escaped my lips. "With all the weird things that have happened, this has to be the weirdest."

"Have your headaches returned?" he guessed.

I shook my head. "No, but-" I jumped as a flock of snowbirds flew out of a nearby tree and headed out over the lake.

Xander smiled down at me. "There is nothing to fear so long as we are together."

MYTHS BEYOND DRAGONS

I looked out over the lake and pursed my lips. "I'm not sure we can do this-" There came the sound of a single drop of water hitting the surface of a puddle. The sound was faraway, like an echo from a distant world.

I froze, and so did the rest of the world. The flock of birds that flew over the lake were frozen in mid-flight. The breeze no longer stirred the bare branches of the trees. The colors became muted, as though someone had taken most of the life out of the world. The cold that had chilled me now sank into my bones.

My shoulders slumped and I pinched the bridge of my nose. "Not again. . ."

Then I remembered I wasn't alone. A smile stretched across my face as I spun around. Xander stood behind me, but he, too, was a muted statue. My face fell. I walked up to him and reached up my hand to cup his cheek.

"Et tu, Xander?" I whispered as I stroked the smooth, warm surface. Wait, *warm?*

His eyes fluttered like he had just awoken and he stumbled forward like a man walking out of a moving vehicle that had suddenly stopped. I caught him before he fell onto the ice and stared up at him with wide eyes.

"You're awake?" I whispered.

He shook himself and raised his head to look at the colorless world around us. "What has happened to Alexandria?"

I steadied him and swept an arm over the timeless area. "Welcome to my world, or what's been my world off-and-on for a few months."

"Is this your old world?" he asked me.

I shook my head. "Nope. Mine had just as much color as yours especially when someone painted their house purple."

"How did we come to be here?" He glanced down at me and tilted his head to one side as he studied my face with a furrowed brow. "Is this some new power you have?"

I cringed. "I hope not, and if it is I don't feel myself using my energy. Besides-" I held up one of my hands, "-no glow."

He raised his eyes to the lake and pursed his lips. "Then perhaps were are in another-" he frowned.

I half-turned and followed his gaze. His eyes lay on the lake. The reflective surface showed the castle. Its colors were as they should have been, but the castle across the lake was the drab one.

"That's. . .that's the castle, isn't it?" I guessed.

Xander nodded. "It is. We are in a reflection of our world." He returned his attention to me and grasped both my hands so we faced each other. "Tell me everything you know."

I shrugged. "It's not that much. I hear this drop of water hitting more water and suddenly everything becomes a black-and-white movie."

He arched an eyebrow. "A 'movie?'"

I shook my head. "Never mind. Everything loses its color and everything stands still."

"And you touched no one else?" he wondered.

I snorted. "I touched everything I could think of hoping it would be my red slippers out of this world, but nothing happened until I tried you."

"Then you had not tried me before?" he guessed.

I shrugged. "I'm not usually in here that long, or even this long. Usually it's just long enough for me to panic and start slapping my hand against walls and people, and then I'm snapped back into the Wonderful World of Color."

"How long have you been coming to this world?" he questioned me.

"Two months."

He frowned at me. "And you spoke nothing of this to me?"

I bit my lower lip and lowered my eyes. "I. . .I kind of thought I was going a little nuts, you know? Like maybe

MYTHS BEYOND DRAGONS

I'd been whacked around a little too much by a Red Dragon and was imagining all of it."

Xander lifted his gaze to the mute world around us and pursed his lips. "Unfortunately, it is very much real, and we are both a part of it for the present."

I smiled up at him. "I'm glad you're the one who's with me. Well, not glad you're with me, but-"

He chuckled. "I understand." He took my hand and guided me toward the arch. "Together we will search the library and contact Apuleius to learn what he may know-" We walked beneath the arch and came out in a whole new world.

We stumbled forward as the incline of the short hill straightened to a flat wood floor. I looked up and saw we were surrounded by floor upon balcony-lined floor of bookshelves filled to the top with books. Far above us was a glass dome that allowed bright light to illuminate the countless floors filled with knowledge, along with a walkway that stretched out from our floor into the void in the center of the circular structure to a free-standing platform that looked out over all of the books.

Xander stepped forward with his mouth agape and looked up at the skylight. "Is this the fabled Mallus Library?"

I followed him and frowned. "Yeah, but how'd we get here without a door?"

"Even an archway is a door to a new place," a voice spoke up.

We both turned to the free-standing pathway to see Crates striding down it toward us. He slipped around the corner and stopped a few feet from where we stood with a smile on his face. His gaze fell on Xander and he inclined his head. "It is an honor to meet the son of Cate, wife of Alexander the Tenth."

Xander arched an eyebrow. "You knew my mother?"

Crates nodded. "Yes. She was very curious and often found herself here in search of answers." He chuckled. "At one point her visitations were so often I wondered if I shouldn't make a room for her."

"So were we brought here so you could give us a book only Tillit can read on how to paint the world?" I asked him.

Crates shook his head. "On the contrary. It is I who need you."

CHAPTER 2

I blinked at him. "Help with what? Dusting?"

All humor fell from Crates's face as he shook his head. "Unfortunately, the favor I ask of you is quite serious. The gods of the world must be returned to their ancient home."

I arched an eyebrow and looked up at Xander. "Have you ever dealt with a god?"

He shook his head. "None but the fae."

"The fae may be immortal, but they are not gods," Crates spoke up. He half-turned back the way he came, but kept his gaze on us. "Come with me. I have something that will explain what I mean."

He led us across the path to the circular platform that hovered over the void in the center of the library. There, on a pedestal with a book stand, lay a large, thick tome. The leather cover was brown, aged by countless years, and its binding was worn from countless uses.

Crates stepped to one side and gestured to the book. "This is of what I speak."

We stepped up to the pedestal and studied the pages. The book was opened to a wide picture in the style of medieval paintings that stretched across both pages. The right-hand page showed scenes of fields of yellow grain, many rivers, thick forests, snow-topped black mountains, a wide desert, and open plains. The areas all came together around a single silver-colored tower of stone.

On the opposite page were human figures all pressed together and facing the other page. They wore white robes and their heads were surrounded by halos. There were men and women alike in the bunch of two dozen people, but they all had the same expression of longing as they gazed upon the beautiful geography.

Xander set his hand over the part of the right-hand map with the open plains and furrowed his brow. He looked to Crates. "Is this not a map of our world?"

Crates smiled and nodded. "It is. All the realms of the dragons and those beyond your control."

I pointed at the figures. "So those are the gods?"

His smile faded as he again nodded. "Yes. They were tempted by the beauty of this world and came down to reside among its inhabitants in the hopes of alleviating their eternal boredom. That is why they descended from their world to this one twenty thousand years ago."

Xander and I started back. "Twenty thousand years ago?" he repeated.

A smile touched the corners of his lips. "In the life of an immortal that is hardly a day, and in their world that is nothing."

"So where exactly *is* their world?" I asked him.

"The world you have glimpsed of late, with all its shades of gray at a standstill, is the one in which the gods reside," he explained.

I winced. "No wonder they like our world."

MYTHS BEYOND DRAGONS

He pursed his lips and nodded. "Yes. Theirs is a dreary world without time or beauty, an empty reflection of all the joined worlds, if you will. That is why this world holds so much interest for them, but their presence causes only harm."

"What harm could they be causing after being among us for so long, and how can we be of use?" Xander asked him.

Crates frowned and raised his hand. The pages of the tome flipped on their own to a spot further back in the book. Another map of our world was revealed to us, but the geography was changed. The plains of Cayden's realm were scorched black by fire. A volcano sat where once the Heavy Mountains proudly stood. The Island of Red Fire was gone, swallowed whole by the ocean.

Xander's eyes widened as he reached out and brushed his fingers over the area that represented Alexandria. The city was a mess of ruins with a tempest in the lake.

I looked up at Crates who studied us carefully. "Is this what could happen, or what's going to happen?"

"It is a possible future should those gods that remain not be drawn back into their world," he explained.

Xander lifted his gaze to Crates and pursed his lips. "How can we do this?"

Crates's eyes fell on me and he smiled. "With your unique gifts."

I held up my hands in front of me. "Wait a sec. You're talking about me going up against *gods*? My little water dragons could barely take out that psycho red dragon!"

Crates chuckled. "The experience on the Island of Red Fire changed you more than you realize. It has granted you with abilities beyond that of a mere half-fae, otherwise you would not have been able to defeat the Red Dragon in his full form."

I wrinkled my nose. "So I'm what? Three-quarters of a fae?"

He smiled and shook his head. "No, you are something more than a mere fae. I believe in your old world it is called evolution, but that is such a poor word. It cannot begin to recall the immeasurable awakening that has occurred within you, and continues to change you." He paused and furrowed his brow. "I believe the term 'transcended' has a better grasp on what has happened to you."

I looked down at myself and frowned. "I hate to break it to you, but I don't feel 'transcended.' Hell, I don't feel any different at all."

He arched an eyebrow. "Not even a little?"

I bit my lower lip and turned away from his prying eyes. "Well, I. . .I've kind of been hearing these voices."

"And?" he persisted.

I frowned and shrugged. "And what? It just sounds like a bunch of people whispering around the corner."

Xander frowned. "For how long have you heard these voices?"

I shrank from his stern gaze. "Since after we fell into that pool. I just thought I was imagining things."

"What you hear are the voices of the gods, noises which are beyond the plain of normal humans, and even many fae," Crates told me.

"So I'm not going crazy?" I asked him.

He chuckled and shook his head. "No."

My shoulders drooped and I let out a heavy sigh. "Well, that's something, but I really don't understand what hearing voices is supposed to do for me."

"They are supposed to help you save the world."

My shoulders fell and my face drooped. "Seriously? Didn't we already do that?"

Crates shook his head. "No, or rather, you saved this world for but a moment. The threat presented by these gods and their destructive power will lead you over your travels and test your strength as nothing else has."

MYTHS BEYOND DRAGONS

"How do these gods differ from the fae?" Xander asked him.

Crates smiled. "Fae are mere children in comparison to the gods. A Mare fae may move the tides and a Rus the wind across the plains of wheat, but a god is capable of upending entire oceans or uprooting the ground to create a mountain."

Xander furrowed his brow. "That is a great deal of power."

The librarian nodded. "Yes, and that is why I ask you to do this terrible task."

I cringed. "There's got to be somebody more qualified than me. You know, like some other god."

He looked past me at Xander and smiled. "There is someone equally qualified."

I looked over my shoulder at my Dragon Lord and arched an eyebrow. "Have you been hearing voices, too?"

He shook his head. "No, nor have I felt any effects from the episode in the pool."

"But you were able to defeat the Red Dragon, he who had fulfilled the tenth generation promise of power restoration," Crates pointed out.

Xander shrugged. "His mother was not a true Maiden so he could not be the fulfillment of the tenth generation."

Crates took a few steps back away from us and tucked the book under one arm as he raised his hands together beside his head. "Then I hope I am not making a horrible mistake." He clapped his hands twice in quick succession.

I heard a flutter of wings above us, and a horrible screech echoed down from the lofty heights of the library. Xander and I tilted our heads back and looked up at the glass domed ceiling. The shadowy form of a familiar beast shot downward toward us.

Xander wrapped his arms around me and pulled me away a second before the beast slammed down on the spot where I had just been standing. Its eagle talons dug several inches into the hard stone floor and cracks spread across the stone to where we stood. The creature raised itself to its full height and glared at us with its bright golden eyes.

It meant death, and that death would be ours.

CHAPTER 3

    I looked at the deep cracks and swallowed the lump in my throat before I lifted my eyes. My gaze met the terrifyingly cold eyes of the griffin. It opened its beaked mouth and let out a squawk that rattled some of the nearby bookcases and their books. The beast stalked toward us. Xander slipped in front of me and growled at the creature.

    The griffin squawked and leapt at us with its claws splayed out. He grabbed the wrists of its outstretched eagle arms and dug his heels into the ground. Its lion hind legs hit the floor and pushed against him so that he slid back. I lunged out of their path and hit the railing hard as the two combatants passed by me.

    I whipped my head to Crates who stood in the center of the end of the platform and glared at him. "Call it off!"

    He smiled and shook his head. "I think you will find this rather interesting."

The screech of the griffin forced my attention back to the fight. The creature had pushed Xander against one of the bookcases and leaned forward so its snapping beak nearly bit off his nose. He clenched his teeth as he turned his head to the side to avoid its monstrous jaws.

"Xander!" I yelled.

A green light appeared around his hands, wrapping them in a bright glow that forced the griffin to lean back away from him. Xander turned his face to stare into the eyes of the ghastly beast, and the color of his eyes was a brilliant sea-green. His hands tightened their grip on the griffin so that the creature cried out in pain. He released it and slipped beneath its long, thick body. In one quick movement he lifted the griffin by its stomach and threw it across the chasm and the long path.

I ducked low as the griffin tumbled over us and crashed into the bookcases. Books toppled onto its head, burying it beneath pages and covers.

Xander held his hands out in front of him and studied them with wide eyes. "By the gods. . ." I heard him whisper.

A soft snort came from Crates. "Hardly."

A shrill screech echoed over the library. The pile of books exploded outward and the griffin raised itself from the mess of paper and leather. It lifted its head and let loose another screech that made the walls and floor tremble.

Xander took a step toward the griffin and curled his lips back in a snarl. His hands at his sides transformed into claws and his wings burst from his back. They were thicker and longer than I remembered.

The griffin spread its own wings and flew across the chasm. Xander leapt into the air and the pair collided above the round platform. The griffin slashed at him, but Xander dodged the blows and gave the creature a few hard punches in the beak. The beast lost its flapping timing and nearly tumbled back. Xander grabbed its long neck and flew downward, slamming the beast into the balcony to our right.

The griffin slowly climbed to its feet, but it wasn't unscathed from the tussle. Its wings were limp and its feathers were ruffled. The fur on its behind had patches missing and its tail hung limp behind it. The injured creature, however, raised its head and spread its wings wide, causing Xander to tense and dig his feet into the floor.

My jaw dropped open when the griffin took a step forward and bowed its head to Xander. He furrowed his brow, but force of habit made him return the gesture. The griffin leapt up into the air and disappeared into the heights of the library, leaving behind a mess of books and feathers.

"What the hell. . .?" I whispered.

A noise in Xander's direction forced my attention back to him. He'd take a step toward me, but lost his balance and stumbled into a bookcase to his right.

His clothes were shredded, but his flesh was unscathed. He took a deep, shaky breath and the glow in his hands disappeared. His wings slipped back into his back and his claws changed back to hands.

I scrambled to my feet and rushed over to his side where I propped him up against me. "Are you okay?" I asked him.

His face was pale, but he nodded. "I believe so."

The sound of a slow clap came to my ears. I turned to see it was Crates who did it as he walked up to us. The librarian stopped three feet away and stopped his clapping as he smiled at my exhausted Dragon Lord. "An admirable fight, Lord Xander. I did not expect you to defeat my champion so swiftly."

I narrowed my eyes at our homicidal acquaintance. "So you were *trying* to get him killed?"

He returned my glare with a smile as he shook his head. "On the contrary, I wished to prove to you both how exceptional was Lord Xander's new skills."

"Was it you who granted me such strength?" Xander asked him.

He shook his head. "It was not I who changed you, but the Sæ. With the powers of your admirable mate-" he nodded at me, "-you were able to absorb the infusion of ancient energy and yet remain yourself, and in doing so *you* became the fulfillment of the tenth generation of Dragon Lords."

I arched an eyebrow. "So you're saying Xander has the power of the ancient Dragon Lords?"

Crates nodded. "Yes."

Xander straightened and turned to Crates with pursed lips. "Then it is with these powers alone that we may defeat these gods?"

The librarian shook his head. "Not merely with your abilities, but with your mortal lives."

I wrinkled my nose. "Come again?"

He chuckled. "Your mortality gives you a strength no god can fathom, for only a mortal can understand what it means to fear death and love life. That strength, that determination to fight against death and love life to its fullest is a power no god can defeat, and you, both of you, hold that power in great quantity."

My shoulders drooped and I ran a hand through my hair. "You've got a way of flattering people into taking suicide missions."

"Then you will accept the task?" Crates asked me.

I pursed my lips and looked up at Xander. "Well?"

He smiled down at me. "It seems the fates have decided to give us another adventure, and-" he held up his normal hand and furrowed his brow, "-I wish to see the extent of this new power so I might control it."

I returned my attention to Crates and sighed. "It looks like you've got yourself a Dragon Lord and Maiden."

He smiled and bowed his head. "Excellent. Now I have something for you. If you will come this way."

MYTHS BEYOND DRAGONS

Xander and I arched our eyebrows, but followed Crates over to one of the long glass cases that lined the center of the balcony. Atop the case was a small wood box, but it was inside that interested us most, for in the glass case atop a velvet pillow lay a familiar sword with a blueish tinge to its thick blade.

"Bucephalus!" Xander whispered.

Crates smiled as he gave a nod. "Yes. I asked Valtameri to retrieve it from the sea and bring it to me." He opened a small panel in the case and drew out the blade which he handed to Xander. "Beriadan himself imbued it with a greater power than before so that its blade is now as sharp as the point of a new needle."

"With this power will Bucephalus be capable of vanquishing the gods?" Xander asked him.

Crates shook his head. "No. Its power lies in protecting others from the gods, especially when placed in your hands. I have something else that will assist you in evicting the gods." He grasped the wood box atop the glass case. It was of a plain birch bark with a hinged lid. He opened the lid and held it out to us. "It is this."

Xander and I leaned forward and looked inside. There, nestled atop a nest of soft, pure white cotton, lay a bell that shone like silver. On its top was a short handle of wood that glistened like polished stone. The light above us caught the smooth surface of the bell and reflected our curious faces.

"Can I try it out?" I wondered as I stretched out my hand.

I yelped when Crates snapped the lid shut inches from my finger. "When the time demands it," he scolded me as he shoved the box into my hands.

I glanced down at the box before I looked up at Crates. "So now that we've got all this stuff what do we do?"

Crates shook his head. "That is a task I cannot help you with. You must decide your own course of action."

"But we know nothing of these gods," Xander pointed out.

"Then you had best start your journey and learn," Crates replied as he stepped toward us. He spun us around, placed his hand on our lower backs and shoved us down the walkway and toward the door that was the typical entrance to the library. "I wish you a good journey, and happy hunting."

"Wait!" I yelped as I dug my heels into the floor. Crates had prodigious strength for an old man so that we continued our slide toward the door. "What do these gods look like? How many of them are there?"

"Five of the gods remain, and they are able to change their appearance so any description I could give you would no doubt prove useless," he told us. "I can, however, advise you to listen to those voices and heed them well."

We arrived at the door which opened on its own. Crates slid us onto a dirty path, and before us stretched the majesty of the lake. We spun around to face him as he stood in the doorway of the temple that graced the small peninsula of the lake.

I hugged the box tight to my chest and glared at him. "Can you even tell us how we're supposed to find them?" I questioned him.

"I would suggest you consult books, ask your friends, or-" his eyes flickered to me and he winked, "-inquire of family members for that bit of information." He stepped back and smiled at us as he grasped the side of the door. "Good day, and good luck." Xander and I jumped when he slammed the door shut in our faces.

I blinked at the doorway before I glanced up at Xander. He held an equally confused expression. "Why do I get the feeling we just got volunteered by a used car salesman to *sell* his cars?" My modern analogy was lost on my medieval Dragon Lord. "Never mind. . ."

Xander grabbed the handle of the door and opened it. Inside was the expected interior of the temple. He shut the door and looked down at me with a furrowed brow. "The librarian is a rather peculiar fellow."

I snorted. "You only know the half of it. Anyway-" I looked down at my treasure, "-he forgot to tell us how to use this thing."

Xander held up Bucephalus and studied the blade. "Both of these fine objects are worthless unless we are able to learn who can lead us to the gods."

"I think that's going to be the easiest part of this mess," I argued.

He arched an eyebrow at me. "Then you know to where we must travel?"

I looked up at Xander and grinned. "He told us to go see family, and for me that's only one person. Are you ready to see your mother-in-law again?"

A sly smile slipped onto his own lips. "She is not an unpleasant face to see, especially as she takes after her daughter."

"Nice save. Now let's go."

CHAPTER 4

"Horses. Always with the horses. . ." I grumbled to myself.

I sat atop a fine gray stallion that trotted down the road to the High Castle. It was several days after our meeting with Crates. We were close enough to the castle that I could see a hint of towers in the distance, so that in a few mile or two we would see if I was right about his hint. Beside me on another fine horse was Xander, and behind us came Darda and Spiros.

Another tinge of pain from my rear made me wince. "What I wouldn't do for some twenty-first century comfort. . ."

"How has travel progressed in my old world?" Darda asked me.

"To the point where you can travel for hours in a comfortable seat or fly anywhere with a good drink beside you," I told her.

MYTHS BEYOND DRAGONS

"I would dearly wish to know the secret for how humans fly and drink without falling," Spiros spoke up.

"They fly around in huge metal machines piloted by humans who don't get to drink," I explained.

His face fell. "I see. How disappointing for these 'pilot' humans."

I laughed and glanced at my Dragon Lord. His lips were pursed as he stared straight ahead. I leaned toward him and leaned across the void between us to poke him in the arm. "You okay?"

"I was just thinking back to our interview with the librarian and his avoiding our most pertinent questions," he told me.

I shrugged. "Maybe he just didn't want to make this god-hunting thing too easy-or easy at all-for us. Or maybe he's testing us so we can fight some inter-dimensional beings next." Xander turned to me and arched an eyebrow. I smiled and shook my head. "Believe me, it's not something we're going to have to mess with. Anyway, I'm pretty sure my mom can tell us something about gods. She's almost one herself, at least according to Crates."

Spiros furrowed his brow. "Gods and fae are not the same?"

I glanced over my shoulder at him and shook my head. "Not according to the librarian. He said fae were immortal, but not gods."

Darda frowned. "What creature could have a greater power than that of the fae?"

"The librarian informed us the gods controlled the natural elements while the faes merely use them in a small way," Xander explained.

Spiros whistled. "That is a great deal of power, and this librarian expects you two to protect the world against them with a sword and that-" he nodded at the small wooden box behind Darda's saddle that held the bell.

Darda fidgeted in her saddle and frowned at the road ahead of us. "Such abominable manners not to inform you of what you needed to know."

"At least it gives me a good excuse to see my mom," I reminded our party as the High Castle came into view.

The majestic former residence of the Red Dragons was empty now but for a small staff of caretakers. They would be taking care of us for the evening, but we first had work to do. We continued fifty yards past the castle and stopped on the road where the ground sloped down into the woods.

Xander and I dismounted, as did our companions. I handed my reins to Darda and Spiros was given charge of his horse. Together we two followed the barely perceptible path that wound its way through the woods. In a few short minutes the way opened up and before us a small pool sparkled in the late afternoon sun.

A few gentle bubbles on the calm surface of the pool heralded my mother's arrival. She rose from the water in all her majestic beauty. Her sparkling eyes smiled at me as she stepped up to the edge and held out her hands to me. "My daughter. It is good to see you."

I hurried over and gave her a hug which she returned with equal effort. "Hi, Mom. Miss me?"

She drew me away from her and studied me with those beautiful shimmering blue eyes. "Always, but I gather from your eyes that you have not traveled such a distance merely to see me."

I winced. "That obvious?"

She chuckled. "Your face hides no secrets, and for that I love you the more."

"Well, to be honest there was something we needed to talk to you about. You don't happen to know anything about gods, do you?"

She arched an eyebrow. "You mean the fae?"

Xander stepped up to stand just behind me and shook his head. "No. The keeper of the Shadow Library has tasked us with overcoming gods."

Her eyes widened and looked from Xander to me. "Gods? Those of the natures?"

"You know about them?" I asked her.

Some of the light left her eyes as she pursed her lips and gave a nod. "Yes. They were those above us of whom we do not interfere. Only my father, Valtameri, would dare their fury. However, that was many thousands of years ago. I have had such little news of them from the waters that I thought they had gone from this world."

Xander stepped forward so he stood beside me and looked my mom in the eyes. "You know where they are?"

She nodded. "Yes. That is, under certain conditions."

"But how?" Xander persisted.

My mom sighed. "As a Mare fae I am capable of feeling vibrations through the water so that I can learn of distant happenings merely by touching the water."

"And these happenings encompass the doings of the gods?" he wondered.

She nodded. "Yes. That is, if they have used their great power, then the waters tell me."

My heartbeat quickened as I searched her eyes. "Can you teach me how to do that?"

She shook her head. "I cannot. Though you are my daughter you are still only half of my lineage, and thus you have not the power."

"Even with her increased abilities?" Xander asked her.

My mom glanced from me to him and back again. "Increased abilities? What does he mean?"

I shrugged. "I kind of got soaked in this gooey water on the Island of Red Fire and-"

She tensed and her hands squeezed mine. "The Ealand of Reod Fyr?"

I nodded. "Yeah, why?"

"The goo you speak of, was it the Sæ?" she persisted.
"Yes, but why?"

She drew me over to a large rock and sat us both down on its flat top. "Please tell me this story, and I will see if I cannot help you."

I told her the long tale of our adventures on the Island of Red Fire and the demise of the last of the Red Dragons. When I finished my tale my mother's beautiful face was a mixture of expressions. There was fear, and not a little bit of interest.

"Have you experienced any effects from the Sæ?" she asked me.

I shrugged. "Well, there are the voices."

She tilted her head to one side and a smile teased the corners of her lips. "Voices? What do they sound like?"

I nodded. "Like somebody whispering around a corner."

The smile slipped onto her mouth. "That is very interesting, and very wonderful, news."

I arched an eyebrow. "I don't see how me going nuts is good news."

My mom chuckled and shook her head. "You are not insane, Miriam, but have achieved a higher state of being than is natural for those who are only half fae."

"So what are they trying to tell me?" I asked her.

She gave a short step back and met my eyes. "Let me show you."

My mom took a longer step backward so that I was forced to step up onto the rocks that surrounded the pool. She continued her move backward, but I dug my heels into the stone. "I'd rather not go for a swim," I told her.

She shook her head. "You will not, so long as you have faith and let me guide you."

I took a deep breath and stepped out onto the water expecting to be resemble a drowned rat. My eyes widened as my foot stepped onto the surface of the water, but didn't sink down. Rather, I walked on the surface and the water tickled my arches. I gaped down at my feet as we walked over fish and reeds.

We stopped in the middle of the pool and my mother moved so we faced each other. She smiled as she stepped away and let go of my hand. I gasped as I felt my feet start to sink into the water.

"Calm your emotions and imagine the water ever beneath you, bending to your will," my mother instructed me.

I took a deep breath and took another step forward on my own. My foot remained above the water. I raised my head and grinned at her.

She knelt in front of me and held her hand out in front of her so her palm hovered over the surface. "Now let me show you how it is done."

My mom dipped her hand into the water and spread her fingers out. The water shifted around her fingers and looped around her hand like my tiny dragons. She held out her dry hand to me and smiled. "Give me your hand, Miriam."

I set my hand in hers. She drew me down so I knelt in front of her and dipped my hand down into the water so she clasped both her hands around mine. The little streams of water slipped around my hand. I clenched my teeth and tried not to laugh as they tingled my skin with their soft touch.

One of them touched me. I gasped as my vision changed. One moment I was staring at the pool of water, and the next I was looking out on a large waterfall. The falling water was surrounded on all sides by huge pine trees so thick I couldn't see more than a few yards into the forest. A small deer strode gracefully through the waters at the bottom as fish swam in the small pools that dotted the gentle slope.

I blinked and the vision disappeared so I was back at the pool. My mother studied me. "What did you see?"

I shook my head. "I. . .I think it was a waterfall."

Her smile widened. "With a deer beneath the falls?" I nodded. "You saw that place because the deer disturbed the surface of the water. The water then carries that disturbance across the land to my pool."

"And this waterfall is where?" I asked her.

"The falls are the gateway to your dragon lord's domain beneath the foot of the Heavy Mountains. What you glimpsed happened there only a moment ago."

Xander started back. "But those falls are a day away, even in flight."

She looked past me and nodded her head at him. "Yes. Though the water itself is slow, its messages travels faster than any creature."

"So if a god uses their powers near some water I can see it?" I wondered.

She nodded. "Yes, though my pool is a poor source of information. It gathers water only from the center of the continent, and even then only from particular points. I have sensed no god activity for quite some time, so you will have to find larger rivers in which to test the waters."

"And how am I going to know where they are? I didn't even know where that deer was," I pointed out.

She cupped my cheek in her hand and smiled. "That is something you must learn on your own, but perhaps some of the maps in the castle of Alexandria will help you on your journey."

Xander nodded. "That is true. There are no finer maps in the world than those stored in the library."

I wrapped my arms around my mom and gave her another hug. "Thanks, Mom. I owe you one."

She drew us apart and studied me with a soft smile. "You owe me nothing, my dearest daughter. I will always be at your service whenever you need me." She paused and pursed her lips. "There is a limit to this power, however."

My face fell. "What kind of limit?"

MYTHS BEYOND DRAGONS

"My small streams are rarely traversed so that you saw only one deer. However, the streams and rivers that travel through the realms of the dragons are very busy. Should you try to read the waters you may experience a great deal more visions than you can handle," she warned me.

"What would that do to me?" I asked her.

She shook her head. "I cannot tell, having never gone beyond my pool. I can only advise you, should you find yourself overwhelmed, to focus on yourself. That will ground you to one location and bring you out of the reading. Also-" she grasped my hands and looked into my eyes, "-under no circumstances must you read the ocean. I have no doubt the strain would kill you."

The color drained from my face. "That. . .that's bad."

A smile slipped back onto her lips. "Yes, but I am sure the waters of the continent will give you the information you seek. Now-" her eyes traveled down my attire, "-perhaps something can be done for your clothes."

I followed her gaze and winced. I wore my old jeans and t-shirt, but their age was starting to show. Darda had patched and sewn to the best of her ability, but their cloth was so thin that they were nearly transparent.

I raised my eyes to my mother's smiling face and sheepishly grinned. "Well, they haven't fall off."

"Yet," Xander spoke up.

My mother chuckled. "You are like your father in regards to clothes, but your mate is right. Fortunately, your increased powers may help in this regards. Do as I do," my mom told me as she spread her arms out. I mimicked her gesture. "Now focus on the water at your feet and imagine it rising up and replacing your weary clothes with new ones."

I closed my eyes and furrowed my brow. A mental picture of my attire came to my mind even as I felt the water beneath my feet stir. Soft, cool threads slipped up my legs. I opened my eyes and looked down.

Small tendrils of water like my dragons slithered up my body. They cut my clothes into pieces and parted the fabric as they climbed, but at each cut they flattened and transformed into a perfect replica of my ruined clothes. In a few seconds I was dressed in a perfect, watery copy of my clothes as I bought them new. The water bundled my torn clothes into a tight bundle that floated beside my feet.

"Wow. . ." I whispered as I touched my clothes. They moved and felt like fabric, and on the inside it felt like I was wearing silk. I looked up at my smiling mom. "So can I change them into other clothes?"

She nodded. "Yes. They will bend to your will and create any clothing you desire."

"I hope this will encourage you to wear a dress," Xander teased.

I stuck my tongue out at him before I returned my attention to my mom. "So do I have to worry about the sun drying my clothes off my body?"

She shook her head. "No, nor the wind blowing the water away or the cold freezing you. Your body itself is the pool, and so long as your body remains as it is the water will not fail you."

I smiled and gave her another hug. "Thanks, Mom," I whispered.

She drew us apart and I detected a few tears in her eyes, or perhaps they were just the water. "Now off with you."

We parted, Xander and I were on our way. Spiros and Darda eagerly awaited us at the road.

"Well?" the captain wondered.

"My mom gave me a neat trick to find a god near water, so now we can track them down," I told him.

Darda arched an eyebrow as she studied my attire. "Is this 'trick' able to change your attire, as well?"

MYTHS BEYOND DRAGONS

I grinned and shrugged. "Well, that's another new trick. Anyway, all I need to do is put my finger in every puddle and stream we find and hope the gods are upstream."

"That could take some time to find them," Spiros mused.

Xander mounted his horse and turned to face our small group. "But we must find them nonetheless. We will return to Alexandria tomorrow and stop at every stream. If nothing is found we will continue the search across the continent until we are successful."

I took the reins of my horse from Darda and looked up at my steed with a sigh. "More riding. . ."

CHAPTER 5

The return journey was a little longer because we had to stop at every river, stream, creek, and overflowing puddle so I could stick my hand into the water. Some of the waters weren't as glamorous as the pool.

I winced as I slipped my hand into the sixth puddle that day. The gooey mud squished around my fingers. I shuddered when something slithered over my knuckles.

My three companions sat on their horses nearby. One of them, Darda, had a frown on her face as she looked down at my hunched figure. "Must she do this for every puddle we come across? It is very demeaning to My Lady."

"Unfortunately, it is very necessary," Xander answered her with pursed lips. "The five gods may be anywhere in the world, so we must check everywhere."

I drew out my hand and flicked the mud off as I stood. "This puddle only goes up to an underground spring, and the only thing in there were a couple of blind fish."

MYTHS BEYOND DRAGONS

Darda slipped off her horse with a handkerchief in hand and pursed her lips as she scrubbed my fingers. "Surely there must be a better way than for My Lady to stick her hand in every muck hole."

Spiros turned his face to Xander. "Would it not be better to try the larger bodies of water first? After all, if what the librarian says is true and these gods are a danger to our world than they are most likely going to cause trouble where they can do the most damage."

Xander furrowed his brow. "What you say has merit

A sly smile slipped onto Spiros's lips. "Merit, sense, and a certain quickness to our otherwise slow speed."

A smile teased the corners of Xander's mouth. "Are there any other adjectives you wish to add?"

Spiros furrowed his brow a moment before he shook his head. "None that quite capture the great weight of those I have already used, but here me out. There is the majestic lake at Alexandria. It is fed by a great number of streams and creeks, and-"

"-and is cleaner than these horse-trodden puddles," Darda spoke up as she finished cleaning my hand so that we both climbed back onto our horses.

Spiros bowed his head to her. "I accept the addition, and say it is certainly a cleaner location to start the search. If such a grand lake holds no clues than flying may be a better option."

A shadow passed over Xander's brow that made me frown, but he nodded. "We will try the lake first, and go from there."

We continued on our journey and I didn't have to stick my hand into any other dirty puddles or quick streams. Unfortunately, my mind was now muddied with thoughts of Xander's dark look.

I sidled up close beside him and lowered my voice. "What's wrong?" He shook his head, but I leaned over and set my hand atop his and caught his eyes in mine. "Tonight. Our tent. Be there and tell me."

He smiled and bowed his head. "As my Maiden wishes."

I slipped my hand off his and gave a wink. "As *Miriam* wishes," I corrected him.

Night couldn't come soon enough, but eventually we stopped and made camp for the night. The fire crackled in the makeshift ring of rocks Spiros had constructed as I wandered over to Xander's and my small tent. It was one of those triangular operations with flaps on either end for privacy. I lifted the front flap and found my dragon lord stretched out on the blankets we shared. It would have been a sensually tempting sight except for the contemplative expression on his face.

"Spiros sure can use his breath to start a fire," I commented as I slipped inside and plopped myself beside him.

Xander nodded. "Yes. He has always had an excellent talent for outdoor activities."

I leaned my back against his stomach and looked him in the eyes. "So are you going to tell me why you suddenly have a problem with flying, or do I have to tickle it out of you?"

He pursed his lips and looked down at the ground. "I do not trust myself."

I arched an eyebrow. "With what?"

"With my transformation."

"With your dragon transformation?" He nodded. I sat up and frowned at him. "But you just did it a week ago in the library."

"It was at that point that I became concerned about my transformation," he revealed as he lifted his eyes to mine. "As a dragon lord I have always known power, but not in the quantity I felt when I battled the griffin."

MYTHS BEYOND DRAGONS

I wrinkled my nose. "But you had that much power when you fought the Red Dragon, and when you fought me in the cavern."

He shut his eyes and turned his face away. "That is what I fear."

"You think you're going to turn into that huge dragon?" I guessed.

"Yes."

I shrugged. "That's fine."

His eyes flew open and he whipped his head in my direction. "You would wish for me to attempt to kill you?"

I snorted. "No, but I beat you before, so I can do it again. You'd just need a good slap across the face with my water powers and you'd be as right as rain."

He arched an eyebrow. "Have you mastered the skill that purifies people?"

"No, but the slapping part should be fun. Besides-" I grinned and playfully pushed against his chest, "-maybe I'll knock some sense into you and you'll remember that I'll never let anything happen to you, and I expect the same thing from you."

A crooked smile slipped onto his lips and one of his arms wrapped around my waist. He pinned my back against his chest and pressed a teasing kiss on my cheek. "My little Maiden. My ever-loving and caring Miriam."

I rolled my eyes, but couldn't hide my smile. "You say that to all the beautiful, adorable-"

"Modest?" he suggested.

"And modest Maidens," I teased.

Xander wrapped both arms around me and drew me down so I was forced to stretch myself out on the blankets beside me. He buried his face in my neck and took a deep breath of my scent. "There is only one Maiden for me."

I turned around and snuggled against his warm, smooth chest. A sigh escaped my lips as I closed my eyes and let myself relax. "Good. I'd hate to have to kill a rival."

He chuckled. The soft vibrations rippled through me. "I would hate to watch such a the pitiless battle."

My face fell and I looked up into his face. "You think we're up for a battle with these gods?"

He pressed me closer to himself and sighed. "I cannot believe they would leave this world willingly."

"Maybe it's as easy as ringing the bell and they leave," I suggested.

"Perhaps, but if the librarian entrusted both of us with this task then he must believe it will not be easy to get so near them," he pointed out.

There came a soft scratching at the front of our tent followed by Spiros's playful voice. "Do not discount your loyal friends so easily, My Lord. We, too, would like a chance to offend the gods."

Xander chuckled. "You will no doubt get that chance, my dear captain, but at this moment not to sleep is our offense-"

"-and tomorrow we do battle with the saddles," I added.

"A good night to you, then, My Lord and Lady," Spiros replied.

"Goodnight," I returned.

"Sleep well, My Lady," Darda called to me.

"Night, Darda," I replied.

I heard our companions retire to their tents. The gentle crackle of the fire and a soft breeze against the side of the tent allowed me to drift to sleep.

CHAPTER 6

A few days later we found ourselves back at the majestic city of Alexandria. It was late morning when we passed through the gates and down the streets to the castle. The shimmering surface of the lake greeted us with soft waves that lapped against the white sands of the banks.

The shuttle ship to the castle awaited us and servants stood on the dock to take the reins of our horses. I dismounted and handed off the reins, but I didn't go down the dock to the ship. My attention lay on those shimmering waters.

I stepped off the start of the dock and walked the short distance across the sand to the blue-green waters of the lake. The waves lapped at my shoes as I knelt before them as though in prayer. That wasn't too far from the truth as I stretched out my hand, but drew it back and bit my lower lip.

Footsteps crunched across the sand and Xander appeared at my side. He stooped and caught my gaze. "Is something the matter?"

I gave him a shaky smile. "I've mostly been touching puddles, so I'm a little-well, a little reluctant to touch this much water. I don't want to see that many deer or have my head explode."

Xander grasped my left and smiled at me. "I will be here to prevent your head from exploding."

I snorted. "Thanks." I stretched out my hand and gingerly touched my fingertips to the water.

The experience was, well, overwhelming. All the puddles and streams ever told me were about rabbits hopping through their waters or deer tramping among the river rocks. They were small stories in the lives of smaller animals.

The lake, however, told me a saga of life. It was like viewing a movie with more characters than a Russian novel and more scenes than an international crime thriller. There were animals in the pictures, but much more than that. Fisherman skiffed across the surface in their boats. Children played in the shallows while their mothers chased after the naughtier ones. It was life. The full, unabridged life of the life-giving waters.

One of those lives stood out from the rest like a a bonfire among matches. The backdrop for the drama was a large lake, larger than the one in which my fingers were submerged. The water was surrounded on two sides by tall, steep mountain walls. Their tops disappeared into thick white clouds, but just beneath the clouds was a dusting of snow.

One of the other sides of the lake was a small, flat plain with a large city, and the other side, on the opposite shore, showed a gap in the mountains through which water flowed. I realized then that there were two lakes separated by those white cliffs, and they shared the same water who's source were dozens of small streams from the tops of the mountains.

MYTHS BEYOND DRAGONS

It was in the second lake that I felt the anomaly. It started out as a ripple without a source, but the ripples grew stronger with each passing moment. The calm surface of the lake bubbled up into whitecaps that rocked the few boats on its waters. The men cried out in terror and clutched the railings as their ships rocked from side-to-side.

The waves stopped as suddenly as they had begun. The ripples I felt disappeared, but left me with a lingering feeling, as though I'd brushed against something greater than myself,and came away with the knowledge that I was a speck in the world.

"Miriam!"

I started back and blinked. The scene of the lakes with their high mountains disappeared. I was back at the lake in Alexandria, and all around me were my concerned friends.

Xander grasped my right wrist in his and little water droplets dripped from my fingers. His eyes searched my face as he pursed his lips. "Are you unhurt?"

I shook my head to clear the foggy thoughts left by the reading and arched an eyebrow. "Yeah, why wouldn't I be?"

"You stared at the water for several minutes without response, and I could not pull your hand free of the water," he revealed.

Darda set her hand on my shoulders. "You should rest now."

I shook my head. "I can't, at least not yet. I think I saw a god."

"Nearby?" Spiros asked me.

I shrugged. "I don't know. I've never been there before."

"Can you describe it?" Xander wondered. I described what I had seen in as great a detail as I could manage. Xander furrowed his brow and glanced at Spiros. "Those resemble the Didymes Limnes."

Spiros nodded. "Yes, but we can confirm that with the maps."

"The what?" I spoke up.

"The name translates to 'Twin Lakes,' and they constitute the northeastern boundary of our realm against that of the Black Dragon," Xander explained.

Xander helped me to my shaky feet with Darda flitting behind me. "Miriam should rest," she insisted.

I shook my head. "I'm fine, really. It was just a lot to take in, that's all."

Xander pursed his lips as he studied me. "Your face is rather pale. Perhaps we should wait."

I snorted. "They're just maps. I think I can look at them sitting down."

A sly smile slipped onto Spiros's lips. "You have not seen the maps of Alexandria, My Lady."

We proceeded toward the ship, but a uniformed officer rushed up on horseback from the direction of the city. He dismounted and hurried over to Spiros to whom he bowed. "Captain, a word from the front."

Spiros arched an eyebrow. "Well, what is it?"

The messenger's eyes flickered over all those present. "The word was sent by special messenger, Captain, and he would not give the message to anyone but you. I have come to take you to the gate tower to hear what he has to say."

The captain of the Alexandrian guards pursed his lips and glanced over his shoulder at Xander. "My Lord-"

Xander shook his head. "There is no need to explain. For the good of Alexandria your duties as her captain must come first. We will meet you in the map room."

Spiros turned completely to us and bowed to Xander. "Yes, My Lord." The captain returned his attention to the messenger, and together the two strode off with the horse.

We three boarded the vessel and crossed the calm waters to the majestic castle nestled against the steep mountain. The servants greeted us at the dock with smiles and bows, and I was glad when they removed my heavy traveling coat and hard riding boots.

Xander offered me his arm. "I do not believe you have seen the map room."

I shook my head as I accepted his arm. "No. I didn't even know there was such a thing."

"It is a source of pride for my family," he told me as he led me down the hall. Darda followed behind us like my shadow. "We have been collecting maps since before our lordship over the realm, first as a matter of military policy and then out of respect for such magnificent craftsmanship." A smile slipped onto his lips. "My father spent a great deal on them, so much so that my mother fretted that he would drain the coffers of the realm."

"He nearly did with one purchase," Darda spoke up.

Xander chuckled. "Yes, but that was not quite so high as the price of another which my ancestor happily paid and which will be the one most useful to us now."

We walked through the tall front doors of the castle and into its marble halls. The tapestries and paintings welcomed us, as did the servants in their crisp, clean clothing. I smiled and bowed my head to them as we passed down the corridors warmed by the sun and the crackling fires in all the principle rooms.

Xander led us through the myriad of halls to a room at the rear and right. A pair of thick wooden doors hid the interior. He opened them and revealed a large room lined on either side with small, square cubby holes of various sizes. In each hole lay a rolled-up piece of thick, and sometimes yellowed, paper, also of different sizes.

On the wall opposite us were several panes of glass that made up a window twenty feet tall and thirty feet wide. The window gave us an excellent view of the sparkling lake and the mountain to the left. Thick red curtains hung on either side of the glass, but were held back by small, thick cords of rope.

In the middle of the room stood a large, long wood table around which were four small chairs. Several smaller tables stood in front of either wall of holes, but those had no chairs.

We stepped inside and Xander closed the door behind us. He strode over to the left wall and inspected the small paper tags that were attached to the ends of the rolled papers. I walked over to the opposite side and looked at the rolls. Ink marks shown through the paper and revealed inked mountains, roads, and cities. It was then I realized they were all maps.

I turned to Xander who drew out a particularly large one. "This is a lot of maps."

He smiled as he set the map he held on the table and pushed one end away from him. The map unfurled and revealed itself to be that of Xander's realm, complete with Viridi Silva with its forest of the elves, the river Potami where I'd encountered my first wet relative, and the fine capital city of Alexandria. Each place was as detailed as an online map image scrolled out for maximum view so that one could see tiny streets of Metsan Keskella and the individual wheat fields that surrounded Alexandria's main gate.

I stepped up to the table and gaped at the intricate ink work. "I can see why this would cost a fortune. It must've taken the mapmaker a dragon's life to draw out everything."

Xander shook his head. "Not nearly that long, and it is not the ink work that made the map so expensive, it is this."

He set his spread hand the city of Alexandria. A transparent image popped out of the map and hovered above our heads. The image was that of Alexandria, and projected her majesty like a hologram from a science fiction movie. It showed every nick on the stone buildings and every winding street that stretched across the grand city.

My mouth dropped open as I watched tiny figures walk to and fro along those very streets. Small carts laden with vegetables rolled past the buildings on the way to the market. Horsemen in the armor of the Alexandrian guards patrolled the streets and warily watched a few drunks stagger out of a pub.

Beneath the whole image was the name of the city in large, cursive letters written in golden ink that glowed like starlight.

I looked at Xander, but pointed at the floating image. My voice came out in a squeaky whisper. "How?"

CHAPTER 7

    Xander chuckled at my surprise. "The cartographer convinced the witches of the Coven Caves in the Black realm to enchant the map with the ability to gaze upon any location in my realm," he explained. He lifted his hand and the image was sucked back into the map.
    "So what we just saw was really happening right now?" I wondered.
    "At this exact moment."
    I leaned back and wrinkled my nose. "So was this map just made?"
    "No. The cartographer-" he tapped on a name scrawled on one corner of the map, "-a dragon by the name of Altair, offered it to my great-grandfather in exchange for a large tract of land that borders the realm controlled by Cayden. My ancestor agreed to the price and the Zoi map has been a closely-guarded heirloom ever since."
    "'Zoi?'" I repeated.

MYTHS BEYOND DRAGONS

He nodded. "Yes. In the native tongue of Alexandria it means 'life,' a reference to both the sacrifice of the cartographer and the gift of valuable property to his heirs from which to this day they still draw their income."

"So if this map was made that long ago how come it's showing us what's going on right now?" I asked him.

"That is part of the enchantment. The map continually updates itself. Even the slightest change-" he set his hand on the Potami River. The fast-moving water came up on the air in front of us, and we were able to watch the erosion of a small bit of dirt as it collapsed into the harsh waters, "-is instantly recorded."

My eyes widened. "Wow. So what else can this baby do?"

Xander cupped his chin in one hand and studied the weathered map. "To be honest Altair was unsure himself with what powers the map was imbued. The witches warned him only that the strength of the map relied on life, and like any other map it could be destroyed by water and fire."

"So did he make any more of these maps?" I wondered.

He dropped his hand and shook his head. "No. The price of the enchantment was the cartographer's own life, or rather a decade of his life to that of every witch who participated in the enchantment."

"And how many helped out?"

"Ten."

I winced. "I can see why he didn't want to try it again. So has anyone else tried to convince the witches to enchant another map? It sounds like each one would be worth a king's ransom."

He shook his head. "No. I have heard that the transfer of the years to each individual witch is a painful process akin to dying, and there has not been a cartographer so dedicated to his work and to his family that he would go through such an ordeal."

"Good point." I returned my attention to the map and swept my eyes over the fine details. My eyes stopped on the northeast corner where the squiggly border was colored black. A large body of water was located against the border. I nodded at the location. "So that's the Twin Lakes?"

Xander nodded. "Yes." He reached his hand out, but paused and smiled at me. "Would you like to work the map?"

My eyes widened a little. "Can I?"

"Anyone may use the map. That is why my family has kept it hidden in the castle among the less enchanted maps," he told me.

I smiled. "Sure. Do I just touch it?"

"Yes. Firmly press your hand over the part of the map you wish to see and the image will be brought up," he explained.

I did as he told me and pressed my hand on the lake. An image of the area popped up. It was exactly like my vision at the lake except I couldn't see past the gap in the mountains.

"Is that what you saw?" Xander asked me.

I nodded. "Yeah. Exactly." My eyes wandered down to the name. Like the previous image of Alexandria, the name glowed a bright yellow and read 'Didymes Limnes.' Beneath that name was the translated title of 'Twin Lakes.' I noticed smaller printed, block-shaped symbols beneath the translated name, and nodded at them. "What's that?"

"That is the name by which the lakes are known in the Black realm," Xander told me. "The dragons there call the lakes 'Siblings,' and in their tongue that is Axim."

I leaned forward and squinted at the blocky symbols. "That's what that says?"

He smiled. "Yes. The residents of the Heavy Mountains have always been secluded so that much of their language, written and spoken, is quite different from that of the other realms."

MYTHS BEYOND DRAGONS

I studied the beautiful, cold waters of the lake and the large city that stood along its shores. The tops of the tall, timbered buildings wrapped in pearl-white stucco were reflected on the smooth surface of the lake. The rest of the reflections were blocked by a stucco wall some thirty feet high that curved away from the water like a skate ramp and blocked the peppering water from splashing the houses. A few breaks in the wall allowed access to long wooden docks that stretched out into the water. Small fishing vessels were moored to their upright posts and rocked along the white waves.

I pointed at the holes that I noticed in the mountains north of the lake. "What are those?"

"Those are the source of the winds, the Thyellodeis Spilies, or Windy Caves," he told me.

"So what's the name of the city?" I asked Xander.

"Psychi which translates to 'Soul,'" he told me. "The name refers to the reflection on the surface of the water. The ancient people of the lake believed that the clear reflections were their souls, and that any unexplained ripple in their reflections would signify their death or a death of a loved one by those who watched over the waters."

I arched an eyebrow. "Who watched over the waters?"

A smile slipped onto his lips as he met my gaze. "The legends speak of the gods of the water."

"But not fae?" I wondered.

His smile faltered a little. "That is what we must prove. I hope a Mare fae will gladly speak with you on the shores, if ever there are any in the lake, and by their help we may find out about this god."

"I am afraid it may be more difficult than a conversation."

We all looked to the door and found Spiros standing in the doorway. His lips were pursed and a shadow hung over his brow.

Xander arched an eyebrow. "What do you mean?"

Spiros turned and closed the door behind him before he returned his attention to us with his grave expression. "A message has been received from the Twin Lakes. It appears one of the princes of the Black realm has taken command of Zem and intensified the fleet-building begun by Herod."

Xander pursed his lips. "I see. Do we know his intentions?"

Spiros shook his head. "No, My Lord, but the smallest ships of the fleet have been seen past the Chasma."

I blinked at the men. "The what? The where?"

Darda came up behind me and her low voice tickled my ear. "Zem is the city on the northern lake that lies within the Black realm, and the Chasma is the gap in the mountains."

Xander's eyebrows crashed down and he narrowed his eyes. "How have we replied to this violation?"

"We have stationed ships near the mouth and the old fortress of Omonoia was taken before the-" he cleared his throat, "-before our competitors could take possession of its strategic position."

"What is the name of this prince?" Xander questioned his captain.

"He is Philip Keper, prince of the eastern countryside while Herod lived," Spiros told him.

"Has he an enemy other than my people that would force him to make these actions?" Xander inquired.

Spiros nodded. "Yes. He builds his forces against his cousin, Salome. As distant relatives of Herod, and the only ones who have survived the paranoia of that family, they are both vying for lordship over the realm."

Xander snorted, but the sound was more bitter than bemused. "The paranoia survives on so long as two of that family lives."

I removed my hand from the map to cross my arms over my chest and glare at him. "Why are you mad about that? I'm the one who was almost executed the last time we visited that black place."

My dragon lord turned to me with a small smile and bowed his head. "I stand corrected, though you were quite courageous against such odds."

"Yeah, well, it was either die trying or just die," I quipped.

"Do you intend to send yourself to the front lines?" Spiros spoke up.

Xander gave a nod. "Yes. Miriam and I have no choice but to travel to the Twin Lakes, though we will do so under disguise so as not to worsen an already dire situation."

Xander glanced between Spiros and my old handmaid. "You will both remain at the castle to manage things during our absence."

Darda puffed out her chest and glared at Xander. "I will not, My Lord."

He arched an eyebrow. "You disobey me?"

Darda pursed her lips. "Begging your pardon, My Lord, but for this one time I must disobey you. I was not allowed to follow My Lady to that horrible island, and she was nearly killed by that beast of a dragon. I will now follow her to the ends of the world-nay, even to the heavens and hells of both worlds so that she will be kept safe."

I looked up at Xander and grinned. "I think that's a 'no.'"

A smile teased the corners of his lips as he bowed his head to Darda. "As you wish." He turned his head to Spiros. "I suppose you also wish to join us."

Spiros held up one of the rolled up maps and grinned. "I would gladly remain at the castle, My Lord, but you are in desperate need of an Odigos or you may stumble into a deadly swamp or an unexpected ocean."

"A what?" I spoke up.

"An Odigos is one who is capable of reading maps," Xander explained.

I nodded at the map. "How hard can it be to read that thing?"

A sly smile slipped onto Spiros's lips as he strode over to the map and swept his hand across a narrow valley that ran from Alexandria northward toward the lakes. The images before had been large and detailed, but merely square in shape and with definite boundaries. Now, though, the image that appeared, that of a dirt path lined on either side by tall, rocky walls, was rectangular with edges that slowly diminished to nothing.

Spiros kept one hand on the map while he reached up with his other and danced his fingers across the image. The five points he touched expanded outward as another five images, and each image showed even greater detail. I could see the individual blades of the mountain grass, the bit of dust kicked up by a small breeze, and even a small, round beetle as it scurried across the path.

Spiros lifted his hand that touched the map and the images sucked back into the paper. He turned to me with his smile. "That is the abilities of an Odigos."

A smile spread across my lips as I clapped my hands together. "Bravo! Encore! Encore!"

Xander chuckled. "As the son of a basket weaver you were always rather skillful with your fingers."

Spiros raised one hand and wiggled his fingers at my dragon lord. "It comes with the territory, My Lord, and I know your territory as well as I know my own."

Xander sighed and nodded. "Very well, you may come, but see to it-" he glanced at Darda, "-both of you, that there are adequate replacements. We do not know how long we will be away."

"How long does it take to get to the lakes?" I asked him.

"Two days of flight and an hour over land," he told me.

I wrinkled my nose. "Why by land?"

Xander nodded at the blue waters. "There are strong gales across those waters that travel overland so that flight is dangerous. It is only recently that even the fishing vessels were able to reliably travel across the water without capsizing."

I winced as a twinge of pain shot through one of my butt cheeks. "We get a day to rest, right?"

Xander turned to Spiros. "How long was the message in waiting?"

"Four days," he revealed.

Xander pursed his lips and glanced over his shoulder at me. "We leave today."

My shoulders fell. "That's what I thought. . ."

CHAPTER 8

We had a short delay to resupply our food provisions and gather some fresh clothing. Darda was adamant she herself pack my things so that I was given a few minutes to walk the halls of the grand castle to stretch my weary, horse-bowed legs. On the higher levels were balconies that overlooked the lake and were also used as platforms from which one anyone with wings could take flight and easily fly over the city.

It was at one of these balconies that I found Xander at the railing with his arms crossed one over the other on the banister. Even from the cute rear I could see his body was tense as he looked out over the lake and his city. I joined him at his side and looked up in his face. His lips were pursed and his eyes unblinking.

"Still worried about flying?" I asked him.

He gave a nod. "I am."

MYTHS BEYOND DRAGONS

I set my hand atop one of his and smiled at him. "You'll be fine."

He looked down at me and studied my face with his beautiful bright eyes. "How much faith do you place in your fae abilities?"

I shrugged. "I guess as much faith as I place in myself. I mean, I can't do any more than that."

"Then you do not worry about losing control?" he wondered.

I winced and turned my gaze to the city. "I didn't say that. I mean, neither of us really know what we're capable of anymore, do we? Maybe I could wave my hand-" I stretched my arm out and waved it at the lake, "-and the whole city might be under-" I froze as a large whirlpool appeared in the center of the lake.

From its depths rose a large water dragon the size of those I'd summoned during our fight against the Red Dragon. It stretched itself upward into the sky and stopped three hundred feet above the water at the same elevation as where we stood. The creature turned to face us and its glistening blue eyes fell on me.

I jerked back my extended arm. The dragon's body broke apart and it dropped back into the water with a heavy splatter. The whirlpool disappeared and the lake resumed its calm surface.

I whipped my head to Xander and nervously smiled at him. "You think somebody noticed that?"

A smile teased the corners of his lips as he nodded down at the lake. "I believe so."

I followed his gaze and watched Beriadan, the fae of the lake and consequently my uncle, rise from the waters. He leaned his head back and frowned at me.

I leaned over the railing and cupped one hand over my mouth. "Sorry!" He shook his head and slid back into the water. I returned my attention to my dragon lord, but my face fell when I noticed his downcast look. I gave his shoulder a little shake. "It's all right. It was just a little-well, a big dragon, but the water's back where I found it."

He shook his head. "I fear my transformation may not be so peaceful."

"You were just fine in the library," I pointed out.

Xander turned his face so he looked into my eyes. "Yes, but I attempted to murder you in that pool area, and to know I am still capable of such an act is-" he turned his face away and clenched his teeth, "-it is terrifying even to think of that possibility."

I grasped one of his hands between my own and gave a tug. He returned his attention to me and I smiled at him. "You've always been capable of doing that."

He arched an eyebrow. "What do you mean?"

I snorted. "I haven't always been this all-powerful, beautiful, talented Mare fae, remember?"

"And modest," he added.

"That, too. Anyway, the first time we met-or I guess it was the first time we were alone-was at my mom's pond. You remember how angry you were with me?"

He nodded. "Yes. I believed you would bring the wrath of the Mare fae on everyone in the High Castle."

"Well, at that time you could've snapped me like a twig and I wouldn't have been able to stop you, but you didn't," I pointed out.

Xander sighed and looked out on the lake. "You are correct."

I frowned. "But you still doubt yourself?" He nodded. A devious thought entered my mind as my eyes flickered to the long drop below us. I released his hand and slipped behind his morose self. "How about I give you a push in the right direction?"

"What are you-" Xander had only a chance to look over his shoulder before I shoved my hands against his lower back.

MYTHS BEYOND DRAGONS

He was a heavy dragon lord, but I had determination behind my push so that he flew head-first over the railing. I rushed to the edge and leaned over the railing to watch him fall head-over-heels toward the ground.

His wings unfurled, their length and thickness greater than when I saw them in the library. He spread them out and caught a updraft from where the lake met the shore so that he flew up like a cannonball fired from an overstuffed cannon. I only had time to lean back before he landed neatly on the wide stone railing in front of me. He clamped his long claws on the inner edge of the banister and knelt low so our faces were nearly even with his hovering only a few inches from mine.

He didn't look happy as his narrowed, blue-green eyes glared at me.

I sheepishly grinned at him. "See? You don't want to hurt me, right?" The muscles on his back legs tensed. I took a step back and held up my hands in front of me. "Right?"

Xander sprang at me. I screamed like a girl and spun around to run inside the castle. He landed behind me and wrapped his arms around me, pinning me to his chest and slightly lifting me off the ground. My feet flailed in the air as I squirmed in his hold.

"It was a joke! I swear it was a joke!" I insisted. A chuckle rumbled out of his chest and vibrated down my body. I paused and glanced over my shoulder. Xander's eyes were still sea green, but there was a devilish grin on his lips. My body drooped in his hold as I glared at him. "That is *not* funny."

His humor didn't drop as he set me down and opened his arms. "It was merely a joke," he teased.

I took a step forward and spun around to face him with my arms crossed over my chest. "It wouldn't have been that funny if I'd died of a heart attack."

"I have faith that my Maiden is stronger than that," he countered.

"Miriam! Miriam!" came the frantic chant of Darda as she rushed onto the balcony. Her back was laden with a heavy bag from which bulged clothing, dried food, and the box that contained the bell. She flew to my side and looked me over. "What happened? What is the matter?"

I looked past her at my mischievous dragon lord. "Xander and I were just having a discussion on the 'till-death-do-us-part' part of the marriage vow."

"Your argument seems to have had a very unique effect on him," Spiros spoke up as he strode onto the balcony. He stopped a few feet from Xander and looked over his fellow dragon with an arched eyebrow. "I had no idea I would have to remind you, My Lord, that dragon wings generally stop growing after the twenty-fifth year."

Xander folded his wings behind himself rather than tuck them inside his body. "They are a side effect of the Sæ."

"Have you any Sæ left?" his captain asked him.

My dragon lord pursed his lips and shook his head. "No. Miriam swept them away so that no one else could abuse that great power."

"Though a little remains within you, My Lord," Spiros pointed out.

Xander nodded. "Yes. It remains to be seen whether that great power will abuse me."

Spiros arched an eyebrow. "My Lord?"

Xander shook himself and smiled at his old friend. "Have you prepared for our journey?"

Spiros stepped to one side and gestured to a pack he'd left near the doorway to the balcony. "Prepared and waiting, My Lord."

Xander turned his attention to me and held out his arms. "Care for a ride?"

I sighed, but couldn't help but smile. "This isn't my first time, but please be gentle."

He chuckled. "Always."

CHAPTER 9

The wind whipped at my hair and the bright sun baked my cheeks as we made our way to the far end of Xander's realm. I was huddled beneath a fine fur coat with Xander's arms beneath that. I leaned to my left and glanced down at the ground that lay some two hundred feet below us.

We were close to the foot of the Heavy Mountains so that the land was peppered with discarded boulders and piles of rubble. Tall, thick forests of pine trees partially hid the rocks, but couldn't hide the many small lakes and ponds that were fed by the tiny, meandering streams that hailed from the mountains. Wild deer drank at the edge of the waters while rabbits, seeing our shadows as we flew over, darted into their rocky burrows.

Our flight path followed a ground path that was cut and hewn from the rough terrain. The trail was as straight as our flying which meant that any boulder in its path had been torn apart and carted out of the way. The trees, too, had been cleared long ago, so long that there were no signs of stumps. The remaining pines had their limbs cut high to avoid anyone hitting their heads, even if they were on horseback.

"That path must've been fun to build," I commented.

Xander nodded. "It was rather difficult, but my great-great-great grandfather, the lord who commissioned its building, insisted the path be as straight as a dragon could fly so that should anyone fall on the journey they could be quickly rescued."

I arched an eyebrow. "Did that happen a lot back then?"

My dragon lord shook his head. "No, but he himself had lost a daughter to this wild area. She had been traveling with some companions when a storm overtook them. In the downpour and lightning she was struck and fell somewhere in this area. A search was made, but her body was never recovered."

I winced. "How awful."

Spiros flew close to us and nodded at the path. "There are rumors her ghost haunts the trail near the outpost."

"What's the outpost?" I asked him.

"The small station where we must land," Xander told me as he adjusted his hold on me. I yelped and tightened my grip around his neck. He smiled down at me. "I will never let you fall."

"It's not you I'm worried about, it's Lady Luck deciding I'd look good as a pancake," I quipped. I took another look at the land beneath us and pursed my lips. "You know, we seriously need to consider getting me Joined to you."

Xander furrowed his brow as he looked ahead. "I am not sure that would be a wise decision."

I looked up at him with a frown. "Why not? Don't you want me to avoid being a hag for a few hundred years?"

MYTHS BEYOND DRAGONS

He shook his head. "We do not know what consequences would arise from such a joining. In the typical case I would merely grant you with my extended life, but as we are now more than merely a dragon lord and Maiden I cannot guarantee there would not be dire results."

My heart sank as I sank in his arms. "I never thought about that. . ."

"There is hope, however," Xander added. I looked up to find him smiling down at me. "Perhaps the librarian, who knew about our conditions, would also know the consequences of our union."

A crooked grin slipped onto my face as I sat up in his arms. "When we get back to the castle we'll have to wish really hard for some help and walk through a random door."

We flew onward until the path below us widened into a large meadow. A dozen log homes stood beside the path with their backs nestled against the forest. A few of the female occupants, dressed in plain brown dresses, swept their front porches with pine brooms, and looked up as we circled. Across the road was a long, low structure some three hundred feet long. Just to the north of the building was a large red barn loaded with hay.

I glanced down at my comfortable jeans and t-shirt. "Well, I'd better get dressed." I focused my mind's eye on what the women below wore, and my clothes changed to match the style. I glanced up at Xander and grinned. "What do you think?"

He smiled and nodded. "Admirable."

We landed, and I saw that three-quarters of the mystery building was a stable. Short, stocky horses were tethered to posts along the entire length of the building. The other part of the structure was an office with some sleeping quarters. Through the grimy windows I glimpsed several narrow beds upon which husky men slept.

A man stepped out of the office and strode over to us. He was a little past middle age with a thick beard and a friendly smile. The man wore a pair of dirty coveralls and heavy pants under a heavy fur cape made out of bear skin. The front claws of the animal acted as clasps to pin the skin to his shoulders.

He stopped in front of our group and swept his eyes over us. "Good morning to you, travelers. Needing-" His gaze stopped on Xander and his eyes widened. "My-"

Xander held up his hand and shook his head. "There is no need of that, Kyrios. As you said, we are merely travelers on our way to the lakes."

Kyrios gathered himself and nodded. "As you wish, sir, but I hope you don't think I'm taking liberties when I say that this woman-" he nodded at me, "-is a very beautiful maiden."

Xander half-turned to stand between the stranger and myself. "Kyrios, this is my wife, Miriam. Miriam, this is Kyrios, master of the outpost and keeper of the path."

Kyrios held out his hand and gave me a hearty shake that nearly crippled my fingers. "A pleasure to meet you, Miriam. I have known your husband for a number of years. He would often come to the lakes in the summer with his family to wreak havoc on the populace with his impish ways."

"Only when the occasion would permit," Xander defended himself.

The master scoffed. "Only when your mother would not be a witness to your devious ways. Aye, and when you brought your friend there was no end of mischief."

Xander chuckled as he gestured to his captain. "I hope few along the lakes have as good a memory and eye as you, Kyrios, or there will be a great deal of panic when they have learned I have brought him with me."

Kyrios looked past Xander at Spiros and a sly smile spread across his lips. "Come to cause another funnel, have you?"

I arched an eyebrow. "Funnel?"

He nodded. "Aye. These two rascals had just learned to use their wings and decided to use them to turn the natural winds that happen along the lakes. To this day nobody's quite sure what happened, but their spinning and twirling over the water created a water funnel some hundred feet tall that threatened to wash away the docks. It was only by the grace of the old king and his guards that the winds were swept back over the lake."

I gave a side-glance at Xander and grinned. "You really tried to destroy your kingdom when you were young, didn't you?"

Xander shrugged. "I can only plead youth for my many escapades."

"They had their own share of help," Darda spoke up. We all turned to her and found her frowning at Kyrios. "The young lord and his captain might not have gotten into such trouble without a guide."

Kyrios rubbed the back of his head and sheepishly grinned. "Darda. As blunt as ever, I see. I must admit I did show the lads a few of the trails along the lake-"

"-and walked them right into Lord Herod's realm," she scolded him with a wag of her finger. "They barely escaped an execution had Lord Alexander not given a king's ransom to free them."

Kyrios coughed into his hand and looked up at Xander. "Yes, well, will you be needing four horses for the trip, or do you two-" he nodded at Spiros, "-wish to share one as in years gone by?"

Xander chuckled. "We would not wish to burden a pony with such weight, so four will do."

"-and make them your gentlest," I spoke up.

"Four of your gentlest ponies, if you would," Xander corrected himself.

Kyrios stepped to one side and gestured to the stables. "I believe I have just the ponies for you, if you would step this way."

I glanced at the long rows of horses. "Are all your horses outside?" I asked him.

Kyrios chuckled as he shook his head. "No. Most of my horses are moving up and down the trail, and I have another, larger stable in Psychi."

"So you just move people up and down the trail?" I wondered.

Kyrios paused in the doorway to the stables and nodded at the higher part of the trail. The path widened to a two-lane dirty road with deep ruts. A line of six wagons, each pulled by four horses, rolled down the trail and stopped at the far end of the stables.

A half dozen men walked out of the stable and up to the wagons. The drivers stepped down and the group all began to unload the crates from the back of the vehicles.

Xander watched the men for a moment before he glanced at Kyrios. "That is a great deal more trade goods than used to travel down this road."

Kyrios shrugged. "The city's grown larger since you last came up here. With the added fish harvest we can barely keep up."

"You do not appear to have enough men to fly the fish down to Alexandria, and I thought most of the trade was traveling from the lake down the Eros River," Xander mused.

"My men can handle it, and the women folk sometimes help, too," Kyrios explained before he jerked his head toward the stables. "But let me show you my fine steeds that I'm sure will give you a smooth ride up the mountain."

CHAPTER 10

He led us into the warm stables where the smell of hay was a welcome relief from the stinging scent of pine. Stalls stood on either side of a wide hall, and I noticed that most of them were empty. Two young men were cleaning out the old hay and putting down fresh beds for the steeds.

The young men glanced up from their work. One of them narrowed his eyes and pursed his lips at us. The other tightened his grip on his broom and looked down at the floor. Kyrios nodded his head at the attentive young man and he resumed his work.

A group of four sturdy horses stood in a long stall chewing a fresh helping of grain. They looked up at us as we approached, and one of them clacked its teeth at me.

I stopped five feet from the stall door and wrinkled my nose at the rude beast. "I don't think that one likes me."

Kyrios opened the stall door and set his hand on the mane of that particular horse as he turned to us. "They might be a little stubborn, but these four are as sure of foot on the path as a dragon's wings are in the sky. They'll get you to Psychi without any trouble."

I reached out my hand to the clattering horse. It whipped its head out and snapped at me. I jerked my hand back and looked at Kyrios. "But will we get there in one piece?"

He chuckled. "Xander will have old Iron-hide. You can have Kyma."

I swept my eyes over the three remaining beasts. "So that would be the man-eating horse, right?"

Kyrios nodded at an old mare that was slowly chewing its oats. She looked to be Methuselah's age and had a sweeping white mark that ran across her back. "That's Kyma. Her back's as soft as a pillow and her lope as easy as a gentle stream."

I walked down the stall wall to the gentle giant and looked her over. Kyma raised her eyes to me and stopped her chewing. I reached out my hand just far enough to cross over the top of the stall wall. She gave a tired old whiny before she nuzzled my hand with her velvety nose.

I smiled and tried not to laugh at the tickling sensation of her wet nose. "I guess this won't be too bad."

Xander arched an eyebrow at my loyal steed before he turned his attention to Kyrios. "This mare has unusual markings. What is her lineage?"

Kyrios shrugged. "That's a bit of a mystery, My-" Xander frowned. Our guide cleared his throat. "That is, sir, I can't really say, but she's sort of a legend in these parts, literal and figurative, that is."

"How?" Spiros spoke up.

"Well, I don't know if you boys remember the old legend about the water mare, do you?" he asked the boyhood friends. Both shook their heads, and he sighed and shook his head. "You two really were wild back then, weren't you?"

"What's the legend?" I asked him.

MYTHS BEYOND DRAGONS

"The legend goes that four thousand years ago-"

My eyes flickered to Xander. "You guys don't do anything small time-wise, do you?" He shook his head before he pressed a finger to his lips.

Kyrios cleared his throat before he continued. "Four thousand years ago an old mare appeared along the shores of the lakes, and behind her came a vast herd of pani, the first anyone had ever seen of them."

"What are pani?" I spoke up.

"A small beast that provides clothing for the cities," Xander explained.

Kyrios nodded. "That, and they graze the weeds on land and by the lakes to nothing so we're not all overran with them."

I pointed at the old mare. "So she's supposed to be this four-thousand year old horse?"

He shrugged. "That's the legend, though this one was found by my dad when he ran the outpost some forty years ago, gods be with him. He was up by the lake when he spotted her near the shore and brought her here where she's remained." He cupped his chin in his hand as he studied the old mare. "Though I must admit I've never seen her take to someone *that* well."

"So what does her name mean?" I asked him.

Kyrios smiled and nodded at her back. "It means 'wave.' My father thought it appropriate considering her strange markings and where he found her walking among them."

"We should be going," Spiros spoke up. "We still have half a day's ride ahead of us."

Xander nodded. "Agreed." He removed a small leather bag from his pocket and handed the container to Kyrios. "I imagine this will compensate you."

Kyrios took the bag and bowed his head as he pocketed the coins. "Very well, sir. Have a good journey."

We walked our horses out of the stables and Darda held Kyma's reins as I put one foot in a stirrup. The mare was so short I only had to do a little hop and I had my other leg over her back and tucked into the loop.

I noticed Darda furrow her brow as she looked at the front of the mare's face. "What is it?" I asked her.

She brushed away the long hair that covered Kyma's upper forehead and arched an eyebrow. "I believe this mare is injured."

Kyrios walked up to stand beside Darda and looked at where she nodded. He smiled and shook his head. "That's nothing. Just an old hard scab."

"Was she clubbed with a round stick?" Darda guessed.

He shrugged. "Nobody can say. My dad found her like that."

Xander mounted his horse and turned to us. "We must hurry or the light will fade before we reach the city."

CHAPTER 11

The ride up the road was as smooth as Kyrios promised as Xander led me, Darda, and Spiros to our destination. Well, except for Xander. His steed lived up to its name as Iron-hide balked at every command. He set the pace, and that was a steady trot that jarred him so hard his teeth chattered like that of his horse.

"How is His Lordship's posterior?" Spiros called from the rear.

Xander shrank down in his saddle and scowled at the mane of his beast. "At this moment my posterior is the lord of my attention, but I should not remind you that you must not refer to me as a 'lord.'"

Spiros chuckled. "Forgive me. Will it be Nester again?"

Xander nodded. "Yes. The name is as good as any."

I glanced up the road. The way was steeper now with large boulders on either side of us. The trees were shorter, but still majestic as they stretched toward the clear sky. A cold wind blew threw me and made me shiver.

I glanced at Xander. "Is this the wind you talked about?"

Xander looked up at the sky and pursed his lips. "Yes."

"It doesn't seem like it could knock a dragon down," I commented.

"The winds are much worse above the trees," Darda spoke up as she pointed at the tops. "See there?"

I followed where her finger pointed. The tops of the trees were only forty feet above us, but they swayed like they were a thousand feet higher than our position.

Xander tried to direct his ornery steed toward the wall of rocks on our right, but he merely reared his head and continued on a straight path. Spiros smiled and moved to the wall where he grabbed a stone the size of his palm. He leaned back in his saddle and threw the stone high into the air. The wind caught the rock halfway up the trees and shoved it to our left and into the forest like the rock was a piece of paper.

My mouth dropped open. "That's a lot of wind."

"Only the rocks on either side of the road protect us from that ferocious wind," Darda explained.

"So how does anyone live on the lake shore?" I asked my companions.

"The large wall that was visible on the map blocks the worst of the wind from the lake, and their boats are now enchanted so that no wind can blow a man off," Spiros told me.

I wrinkled my nose. "That sounds like a lot of trouble to live by a lake. Why do they do it?"

Spiros smiled. "Stubbornness is bred into the people of the Twin Lakes area, and then there is the fish. There is not a finer species of fish in all the world that compares to that which can be caught in the lakes. The locals use it in their delicacy, a strong-tasting fish sauce."

I arched an eyebrow. "Is it any good?"

"It is a taste that must be acquired," he admitted.

I shifted in my saddle. Kyma glanced over her shoulder at me and seemed to raise an eyebrow. I sheepishly grinned at me steed. "Sorry. Soft tush." The horse snorted and resumed its frontward attention. "So how long until we get to the city?"

"A few hours yet. We will reach it by early evening," Xander told me.

The hours passed along like the boulders on either side of us, and eventually the steep path flattened and widened. The trees cleared and a small landing of rocks allowed us to stop and give me my first real glimpse of Psychi.

The city of white stone stretched out below us, nestled as it was in a small depression hardly higher than the lake itself. Our view was of the south side of the city with the lake to the east, or our right. A simple arch of huge timbers stood some hundred yards from our location and was the starting point of the stone roads that made up the streets of the city. Even from that distance I could see that on either side of the roads were long ditches that ran into grated holes.

The buildings were made from the timber and protected from the violent winds and spray by white stucco. The walls of a few of the structures were chipped in places and revealed their brown interior, but otherwise the city was pristine. The early evening sunlight from the east glistened off the one-to-two floor buildings and revealed many long flower boxes that hung just outside the windows.

Beyond the city and to the left was a clear-cut plain nearly as large as the city. Corrals built of the cut trees criss-crossed the area and captured thousands of sheep within their folds. Countless young men were perched on the upright posts of the fences with long, crooked staffs on their hands. Most watched the steep hill that lay on the opposite side of the plain from where we stood while others looked toward the forest.

Xander glanced at Spiros. "Are the wolves still a problem?"

Spiros nodded. "Yes. Lord Herod managed to keep their numbers low for the sake of his own herds, but since his death there has been nothing to stop their breeding and raids."

"Are they in danger of overrunning the herds?" Darda wondered.

The captain shook his head. "No, at least not at the present, but as you know the city has no other food supply other than the fish and the few vegetables they grow in their flower boxes."

I leaned forward and squinted at the sheep. My eyes widened as I beheld a single horn that sprouted from many of their foreheads. "Are those the pani Kyrios was talking about?"

Spiros nodded. "Yes. Because of their horn they are rumored to be related to the naqia, but no one has yet proven the familial connection."

I glanced at Xander. "And pani means-?"

"Cloth, from their fine-" Xander's steed interrupted his explanation with a snort. He jerked backward as it trudged forward down the path. He pulled back on the reins, but the stubborn animal continued its cantor toward the city. "It appears my beast wishes for a warm stall."

Darda shivered and looked up at the trees. The wind was closer to us now so that I felt the hard, cold air atop my head. "I agree with the animal. Let us go on." We proceeded down the gentle slope that led to the city.

"So what does pani taste like?" I asked my companions.

MYTHS BEYOND DRAGONS

Xander shook his head. "No one knows. It is forbidden to eat them as they are considered sacred to the lake."

I glanced to my left at the vast herds. "That's leaving a lot of meat on the bone."

The archway was manned by four guards who sported the green-blue colors of Xander's kingdom. Each of them held staffs similar to the shepherd staffs, but with a sickle on the top.

One of them stepped forward and held up his hand. Xander's steed was at least a law-abiding animal and stopped so that we caught up with him. "State your business," the guard demanded.

"We wish to view the lake and to taste the legendary fish sauce of Psychi," Xander told him.

The guard's narrowed eyes flickered over us before they stopped on me. "Why do you bring a human?"

Xander gestured to Darda. "She is a servant to my mother."

My eyes widened. "I'm a-" Darda slapped one end of her reins across my back.

"How many times must I remind you not to speak unless spoken to?" she snapped.

My mind finally caught on to the ruse and I shrank from her pretend fury. "Sorry, My Lady."

The guard stepped to one side and jerked his head toward the city. "You may enter, but don't let us catch you going toward the other lake or you'll be thrown in the thalassa cell."

Xander nodded. "Yes, sir. Good day."

We trudged forward into the wilderness of the tall buildings. The streets were wide and straight, and many carts and people passed us. The citizens were dressed in thick wool dyed bright red, yellow, and even green. The women wore colorful dresses with sashes around their waists while the men sports loose-fitting pants and vests over their equally free shirts. We passed by many carts laden with fresh fresh. I wrinkled my nose as the scent of such a catch tickled my nostrils.

I waited a full ten seconds before I whipped my head to Darda and frowned at her. "Did you have to hit me so hard?"

"I had to make it believable," she pointed out.

"My back certainly believes it," I quipped as I tried to rub the sore spot. My hand wouldn't quite reach so I dropped my arm and turned my ire on Xander. "And what's with those guys hating humans? I thought this realm had a non-douchebag policy."

Xander arched an eyebrow. "Douchebag?"

"Impolite ass," I rephrased.

"They are afraid," Spiros spoke up.

I turned in my saddle to glance at him. "How can you tell?"

Spiros lifted his eyes to the balconies above us. Many of the windows were shut. A few curious children looked out as we rode past, but quickly hid themselves when they noticed our prying eyes. "I have traveled her many times over many years, but I have never in all my visits seen so many closed windows."

"So what are they afraid of?" I asked him.

We slowed to allow two carts to pass and Xander sidled up to me. "The military might of Herod's former forces, even split between his two heirs, is considerable. Were the young Philip, with the full might of Herod's forces on the lake, inclined to attack the city the citizens would be forced to surrender or risk complete destruction."

"But you-um, but Lord Xander would come save them, right?" I persisted.

He nodded. "Yes, but it would be a terrible war the likes of which no dragon of this age has ever seen."

I winced. "Sounds like that 'thalassa cell' would be really busy. What is it, anyway?"

MYTHS BEYOND DRAGONS

"It is a half dozen cells hewn from the rocks along the northern shore that is half-filled with water from the lake," Xander explained. "The dank, dark confines are very uncomfortable."

"We very nearly experienced them ourselves," Spiros spoke up.

"With the tornado incident?" I guessed.

He smiled and shook his head. "No. Nester here was curious to see what they looked like, so we climbed over to the rocks that overhang the cells. The cells, accessed from the top, are kept open when not in use to avoid trapping any fish during high tide. The slippery rocks meant our footing was not so sure. One of my feet flew out from beneath me and I fell over the edge. Nester caught my hand, but could not find anything on which to hold so that we both fell over the side. Fortunately, a sus had followed us and caught the back of Nester's shirt with his hooked walking stick and pulled us to safety. He was well-rewarded by our fathers and was able to set up quite a successful trading business."

I arched an eyebrow. "I wouldn't happen to know this sus, would I?"

Xander shook his head. "No, but he was the grandfather of-"

"Me."

CHAPTER 12

We all looked to our right where a small, narrow alley met the larger road. Standing in the mouth of the alley half-hidden by the lengthening shadows was none other than Tillit. He was dressed in his usual attire with his trusty bag at his side and the strap slung across his broad chest.

The jolly pig-man had a smile on his tusked face as he bowed his head low to Spiros. "I'm glad to hear you have not forgotten my family's kindness to you, my dear captain."

Spiros grinned at him. "It was a solid investment on the part of your forbearer."

Tillit wagged his finger at the captain. "It was an act of kindness, good captain. Tillit's grandfather was-"

"Tillit," Xander spoke up. The sus turned to him and his grin widened, but my dragon's lord's lips were pursed as he studied our old friend. "What has brought you to Didymes Limnes?"

"Business, and a chance to see some old faces," Tillit admitted.

Xander frowned. "Is it business with Philip?"

Tillit wrinkled his piggish nose. "The ruler of the Zem? Tillit is disappointed My Lord would suggest such a thing."

Xander pressed a finger to his lips and shook his head. "While I am here I am a lord of nothing save my own fate, and my name is Nester."

Tillit's face fell. "An alias in such a peaceful land?" His sad eyes fell on me, and he walked up to stand beside the head of my mare and looked me in the eyes. "Tell this old sus you haven't come to find more adventure."

I winced. "Well, we're not *exactly* on an adventure, more like a-well, more like a-"

"-an adventure?" he finished for me. I nodded my head. The sus bowed his head and sighed. "I see. So Tillit has gotten himself into your next adventure."

"You needn't remain with us if you do not wish it," Xander told him.

He shook himself and puffed out his ample chest. "I could not leave Nester, even if he should command it. No, I'll stick with you and see this trouble through to the end."

Xander swept his eyes over the street with its busy traffic. "I hope to find your concern unnecessary, but until that's proven right or wrong we need a place to stay."

Tillit grinned. "Then let Tillit invite you to his family home. It's not much, but you won't be bothered."

Xander smiled and nodded his head. "Excellent. Lead us there."

Tillit half-turned and jerked his head down the alley behind him. "This way."

We followed Tillit, though the tight confines forced us to dismount and lead our horses. It was in that alley that I realized the importance of the ditches on either side of the main roads. Water ran down the rocks that made up the ground of the alley, but since there was no ditch they had, over countless years, created deep indents in the rocks that were now sizable puddles. I hopped and side-stepped the mess, and wrinkled my nose at the murky brown water.

"Why's it so wet here?" I asked my companions.

"The spray from the lake constantly covers the city," Xander told me as he pulled his snappy steed along. "The water allows the plains to the west to remain green most of the year, but the city is required to have a complicated drainage system so as not to sink into the naturally wet land."

"So we're walking on a swamp patched over with rocks?" I guessed.

He nodded. "Essentially, yes."

Tillit glanced over his shoulder and smile at us. "A lovely place to have another adventure, isn't it? So what's in this new trouble? More Red Dragons? Or perhaps a rogue fae?"

"Neither," Xander replied as he glanced around us. The alley was empty and there were few windows on the tall walls on either side of us. What there were were shut. "We are here at the behest of the Mallus Library to return a god to their realm."

Tillit stopped and turned to us with an arched eyebrow. "A god?" Xander nodded. Tillit whistled before he continued our walk down the alley. "Your talent for trouble is certainly improving, Nester." He glanced at me and smiled. "I think it might have something to do with your beautiful Miriam."

My face fell and my eyelids drooped. "That's not a compliment."

Tillit bowed his head. "A thousand apologies, Miriam, but this way or we won't reach my home before nightfall."

We resumed our walk forward and approached an intersection where the alley was crossed by another wide street. The street lay at an angle that descended toward the lake. We'd hardly reached the crossing points when the sound of shouts and hurried, heavy footsteps interrupted our journey.

I looked down the street and watched a young girl run up the road. She was sixteen with startling white hair that flew two feet behind her. Her pale feet were bare and muddied by the alley. In her arms she clutched a long loaf of bread to the front of her yellow dress. Her face was pale and her eyes wide as she struggled up the slope.

Twenty feet behind her were two men in identical uniforms to the front gate guards. They, too, held the sickle staffs. "Stop, thief!" one of them shouted.

The girl looked over her shoulder at her pursuers. That was her fatal flaw as her feet stumbled over the uneven street and she fell hard onto the muddy ground. The girl tucked the loaf of bread against her chest with one arm and crawled backward with the other as she watched the men close in on her.

I shoved my reins into Darda's hands and rushed forward past Xander and Tillit. "Miriam!" Xander called to me, but I didn't stop until I reached the girl's side.

The men reached the young girl, and one of them held up his sickle. I slid down on my knees and dipped my hand into the many puddles. Little water dragons sprouted from the murky water and shot out at the guards. Their lithe bodies wrapped around the one with the raised sickle and pinned the weapon, and his arms, to his sides.

I slid to a stop beside the girl and wrapped my arms around her shivering form before I glared up at the remaining guard who gaped at his trapped companion. "Don't you guys know how to treat a lady?"

The guard clacked his mouth shut and whipped his head to me. He pointed the sickle end of his staff at the girl and me, and snarled. "Release him, witch!"

Xander rushed between us and held his hands out in front of him toward the guard. "You must excuse my friend! She is a little excitable!"

"Let him go!" the guard insisted.

I pursed my lips, but glanced at my little dragon pets. Their bodies fell apart so that they splashed onto the ground as mere puddles of water. The once-captured guard stumbled back and clutched his sickle to his chest.

"Now hand over the girl!" the guard demanded.

"What has she done?" Xander asked him.

The guard sneered at the dragon lord. "Only stolen a loaf of bread from a respectable baker, now both of you stand back or-"

A pot-belly man of middle age hobbled up the slope and stopped at our little group. The man wore a white apron spattered with flour over his plain brown shirt and pants. His face was red and sweat ran down his brow. He clutched his chest and bent over in a vain attempt to get air into his heaving lungs.

"Where. . .where is she?" he gasped. The guard gestured to the girl beside me. The man straightened and glared at her. "Give me back that loaf of bread, you thief!"

She shrank from his harsh tone, and her own voice was hardly above a whisper. "B-but I paid for it-"

"*Paid* for it? With *this*?" the man shrieked as he fumbled around in his pockets before he drew out a coin, "-this is useless! More than useless! It wastes space in my pockets!"

Xander arched an eyebrow before he held out his hand to the baker. "May I see that?"

The man whipped his head to the dragon lord and glared at him. "Who are you?"

"A collector of antiques, and I believe what you hold there-" Xander nodded at the coin, "-is a very rare item."

The baker turned his nose up at Xander. "What business of yours." His eyes flickered to me and his frown

MYTHS BEYOND DRAGONS

deepened before he returned his attention to Xander. "You're a friend of hers, aren't you? You're trying to trick me into taking a worthless coin, aren't you!"

"Somas!" Tillit yelled as he walked up to our group with open arms. He embraced the baker in a tight hug that made the man blush.

The baker threw the sus off him and glared at Tillit for a moment before the light of recognition lit up his eyes. "Tillit! My goodness, but you frightened me! I thought you were another thief!"

Tillit shook his head and clacked his tongue. "My good Somas, you're far too frightened of thieves."

Somas frowned and jabbed a finger at the girl and me. "Tell that to them! Thieves, both of them!"

Tillit held out his hand. "Mind if I see that coin?"

The baker furrowed his brow, but clapped the coin into the sus's thick palm. "Very well, but only because it is you, Tillit."

Tillit bowed his head. "I'm glad you trust me so." He turned around and presented the coin to Xander. "If you would appraise this coin for me, Mr. Collector, we can agree on its value."

Somas's mouth dropped open as Xander took the coin and studied it. He whipped his head to Tillit and pointed at Xander. "Y-you know him?"

Tillit nodded. "Very much. He's a prolific collector of antiquities." He gestured to Darda. "Even with his servants." She narrowed her eyes at the sus, but said nothing."

Xander turned the coin over and smiled. "As I thought. This is a very rare coin. It was minted to commemorate the peace treaty signed by the two nations of the Black and Green realms some two thousand years ago."

Somas's mouth dropped open. "*It is?*"

Xander nodded. "Yes. I doubt there were more than a hundred made. They were given to the important guests at the ceremony that broke the ground for Omonoia. What makes this even more rare is half were lost in a gale as it tried to reach the Chasma." He glanced down at the battered loaf in the girl's arms and smiled. "I would say she not only deserves that loaf, but-" he turned his attention to the baker, "-she paid you enough to buy your business."

Somas straightened and cleared his throat. "W-well, if that's the case than I will be quite content to take the coin-"

"-and apologize," I spoke up.

He glared at me. "How was I supposed to know the coin was worth that much?"

"Through an old trick," Tillit suggested as he took the coin and clamped it between his teeth. He tried to bend the coin, but only ended up scratching the surface. Years of grime were worn away by his teeth so that the shimmering color of gold shone through. He handed the coin back to its new owner.

Somas gaped at the beautiful yellow metal. "By all the gods."

Xander turned to the guards who held their weapons upright at their sides. "I believe your work here is finished."

They glanced at one another before the leader looked to Somas. "Is everything all right, sir?"

Somas nodded. "Oh yes, very much so. Thank you for your help." The guards bowed their heads and walked back down the gentle slope.

Tillit slipped his arm around his old friend and turned Somas in the same direction. "A pleasure seeing you again, my dear Somas, and should you need my assistance again don't hesitate to call."

"Thank you, and-" he glanced over his shoulder at the young girl, "-my sincerest apologies, young woman. I meant no harm."

I helped her to her feet and she shook her head. "It's fine. Thank you for the bread."

Somas bowed his head to her and waddled back to his shop.

CHAPTER 13

We were left alone with our newfound friend. Xander stepped up to her as I stood by her side and smiled at her. "I am sorry circumstances were so against you. Generally the citizens are not so suspicious of each other."

She shook her head. "It's fine. I'm just glad my coin was worth enough for this bread."

"How did you come by it?" Xander asked her.

Her eyes flickered away from him and she bit her lower lip. "I. . .I found it in the lake a long time ago."

"Near the Chasma?" he wondered.

She shook her head. "I can't remember."

"Nester, we still have company," Spiros spoke up as he swept his eyes over the area. A few curious faces peeked out from behind the window shutters and curtains.

The young woman clutched her bread to her chest and half-turned away from us. "I should go. . ."

"Can we escort you to your home?" Xander offered.

MYTHS BEYOND DRAGONS

She cringed. "I. . .I'm staying with someone else right now."

"What street?" he persisted.

"On Moira Street, but I wouldn't want to trouble you," she argued.

Tillit grinned. "There's no trouble. Moira Street is just around the corner from my house."

She shook her head. "I still don't-"

I looped my arm through one of hers and studied her pale face. "Come on. Your legs are shaking so bad you can barely stand on your own."

She glanced down at her wobbly limbs and sheepishly grinned up at me. "I. . .I guess that frightened me more than I thought."

"Then we'll take you home," I insisted as I guided her down the road.

"Miriam," Tillit called. I paused and glanced over my shoulder. He had a grin on his face as he pointed at the other half of the alley. "It's this way."

I frowned. "I knew that." Out of the corner of my eyes I noticed a ghost of a smile on the young girl's face. I turned us around and marched toward the alley. "*Now* we'll take you home."

Tillit slipped in front of us and Darda managed my steed as I walked arm-in-arm with the young girl. She stared straight ahead, but snatched little glances at me.

"So what's your name?" I asked her.

She shrank down into herself. "I don't think I should-"

"Mine's Miriam," I told her.

She sighed and looked away from me. "It's Helle."

"That is a rather ancient and little used name," Xander spoke up from where he walked behind us.

She shook her head. "I don't know about that." Her eyes flickered to mine and she studied my face with a tense expression. "Are you. . .I mean, are you a fae?"

81

"Half fae," I corrected her.

Her eyes lit up. "Then you are a Mare fae?"

"Guilty as charged."

She tilted her head to one side and furrowed her brow. "But if you're half how can you have such power?"

I shrugged. "I'm a little special."

Xander arched an eyebrow as he studied the young girl. "Are you familiar with fae?"

Helle blushed and shook her head. "No. That is, I *am* interested in them. They-well, I feel very close to them."

"I see." His eyes traveled down to the bread in her hand. "The loaf will hardly last you a day. Would you like us to buy more food for you?"

She shook her head. "Oh, no, I need nothing, but-if it's not too much trouble-I'm sure Agatha would want something to drink."

"Who's Agatha?" I asked her.

She held the bread out in front of her as she walked and smiled at the food. "She is why I bought this. She's a young girl I found alone on the streets after I-well, I found her two months ago." Helle's face fell and she clutched the bread to herself again. "I had some provisions with me, but they ran out a week ago. She was so hungry, and I knew that coin was worth something, so I thought I might trade the metal for food. The man was very kind until I walked to the door with the bread. Then he shouted at me and I-well, I was so frightened that I ran away."

Tillit chuckled. "A natural reaction, especially when the shouter is someone as big as Somas."

Spiros pulled off one of the water packs that hung from the saddle of his steed and held it out to Helle. "I hope this will work for Agatha."

Helle smiled at him and accepted the water. "Thank you, I'm sure she will be grateful."

Spiros bowed his head. "It was my pleasure."

MYTHS BEYOND DRAGONS

My eyes flickered between the pair. Helle blushed and Spiros hardly blinked. I cleared my throat and they started back. "So why don't you just get water from the lake?" I asked her.

She winced. "I. . .I don't like the rough seas. They scare me."

"But you got that coin from the lake," I pointed out.

Helle turned her face away and bit her lower lip. "That was a long time ago, in a time about which I would rather not speak."

I squeezed her arm and smiled. "Then we'll speak of the present. How old are you?"

She blinked at me before she glanced down at herself. "I. . .I think I'm sixteen."

"You don't know?" I wondered.

She shook her head. "No. I lost track a long time ago."

Tillit rubbed his chin as he looked thoughtfully at the alley head of us. "An orphan, eh? Maybe you're a castaway."

I arched an eyebrow. "Castaway from what?"

He waved his hand toward the lakes. "From Herod's realm, or what used to be his realm. He never let anyone come over from Zem except authorized traders and the forests are full of wolves, so sometimes families would try their luck with the water at night." He glanced at Helle and his face fell. "A lot of them didn't make it, or sometimes just one or two."

I glared at the wet ground. "Damn Herod. . ."

Tillit snorted. "The gods are probably giving him his just rewards, but he left enough of a mess for the living to still be a nuisance."

"Have you heard anything of what is going on at Zem?" Xander asked him.

The sus pursed his lips and shook his head. "Not much, but I've heard enough to know it's not good. That Prince Philip, as he styles himself, is gearing up to fight his cousin, Salome, any day now. She only has control of the calvary, otherwise the war would've already started."

"Who would you bet on to win?" Spiros spoke up.

Tillit shrugged. "I don't know. One's got the impenetrable city-fortress of Zem and the other has Herod's fortress-palace. If they met on the open field, I'd place my bets on Salome, but I wouldn't count on Philip to do something that stupid. Salome has some brains, and some beauty, or so I've heard, and won't try her luck on the water."

"Then they are at an impasse," Xander mused.

Tillit nodded. "Yeah, unless one of them gains an ally or Omonoia."

Xander arched an eyebrow. "How can that fortress help either of them?"

Tillit glanced around at the empty alley and lowered his voice. "It's only a rumor, but I've heard that Salome has a crazy plan for Omonoia. The Eros River flows out of the lower lake, this one. The upper lake near Zem doesn't have that big of an outlet so most of its water flows into the lower lake and out the river. If someone was to shut off that flow-"

Xander's eyes widened. "-or block it."

Tillit nodded. "Yep."

I raised my hand. "You lost me."

We reached another intersection of a major road, and Xander looked ahead of us down the street. The road had ended its serpentine shape and now traveled straight toward the lake. A large white wall protected us from the worst of the winds, but a chill breeze and a few loose sprays of water still hit us. The rolling surface of the water stretched out for several miles before it reached the tall Chasma with its wide gap in the rocky, barren mountains.

"If the Chasma were to collapse and seal off the flow of water then the upper lake would flood backward, drowning the city of Zem," Xander explained.

MYTHS BEYOND DRAGONS

The color drained from my face. "How many people live there?"

He shook his head. "That is difficult to discern, but I doubt less than a hundred thousand."

"Jesus. . ." I muttered.

Xander glanced at me and arched an eyebrow. "What is this 'jesus?'"

I shook my head. "It's nothing. Anyway, what do we do first? Stop the Black dragons or the god?" I noticed Helle started back and her eyes widened. "Are you okay?"

She clutched the bread and water bottle to her chest and shook her head. "I-I'm fine. I-I just remembered I really should get home before dark. Agatha might worry about me."

Spiros stepped up beside her and smiled. "Then let us hurry and escort you home." She blushed and averted her face from him, but nodded.

Someone tapped me on the shoulder, and I turned to find Darda holding out my reins to me. Kyma dug her hoofs into the ground and snorted loudly as she tried to break free, but Darda's dragon strength kept her in place.

"If you would take your difficult steed," Darda requested.

I grasped the reins and the animal immediately stopped its struggling. Its soft brown eyes looked into mine like a child finished with its tantrum after its mother arrived.

I grinned at Darda. "All you need is a little tender care."

Tillit snorted. "And a lot of luck, now off we go."

We abandoned our alley-going ways and walked down the street. Soon the smell of fish and water-logged cages and nets filled my nostrils, and the jovial sounds of shouting men reached my ears. A gap in the wall appeared and the full bank of the lake came into view, including the long docks I'd seen in my water reading. The jumble of planks were crowded with burly men who lugged their catch onto the wood, splashing water about as they gave or received orders.

The wind blew off the lake and cut through me like a knife. I wrapped my arms around myself and shivered. "Nice wind. Does it ever stop?"

"Only before an even greater gale," Xander told me.

"Has it always blown?" I wondered.

He shook his head. "No. There are stories from the ages of my ancestors that speak of calm summer days. It is only in the last thousand years or so that the winds have become nearly unbearable and the wall was erected."

"Only a thousand years. . ." I muttered.

Tillit, in the lead, stopped two short blocks from the waterfront and spun around to face us with a big smile as he gestured to a small side street to his right. "We're here!"

CHAPTER 14

The street was narrow with most of the buildings being houses of two floors. The buildings were small, hardly more than twenty feet wide and that tall. Laundry hung from tiny window to opposite window and blanketed the sky in blankets and wet clothes. A few bits of trash littered the otherwise clean but wet cobblestone ground.

I looked down the unprepossessing street with its tight quarters and peeling whitewash walls and wrinkled my nose. "This is-um, nice."

Tillit winked at me and took a step toward the narrow street. "Don't judge too quickly. Just follow Tillit."

We followed the bemused sus one at a time down the by-street. Helle walked behind me. I glanced over my shoulder and noticed that Spiros followed her. He studied her with an attention bordering on rude if there hadn't been a soft, admiring look in his eyes. I smiled and looked ahead.

Tillit led us through the winding street to a two-floor house with an attached stable. He turned to us and grasped the sliding door that led into the beast building. "Welcome to my humble abode."

He slid the door wide open and revealed a whole other world. The inside of the stables had raftered ceilings that were short, but the depth of the building made up for the lack of head space. The stables were twenty feet wide, but fifty feet deep. The stalls stood on the left and the tack hung on the right-hand wall. Beyond a ten-foot long bench on the right near the door was a door that led into the house.

"I own the other buildings on the adjoining block and gave the stables and house a little more room," Tillit explained to our gaping faces.

Darda turned up her nose and frowned. "It will do."

Tillit grinned and bowed his head. "I'm glad you approve, dear Darda, because I'm giving you the stall at the end."

A snort escaped Xander's lip's before he gathered himself. Darda balled her free hand into a fist and glared at the sus. "I would rather sleep in the street than under your roof."

Xander chuckled. "Thank you for the accommodations, though I am sure we would all rather sleep in a bed."

Helle bit her lower lip and took a step away from our group further down the street. "I should probably leave. . ." The young woman backed up right into Spiros's arm.

She looked up and blushed as he smiled down at her. "I am sure our friend Tillit would be glad to treat you to some dinner along with your friend," he offered.

She shook her head. "No. I-"

"Helle!"

We whipped our heads in the direction Helle had tried to escape. A young girl of eight with bouncing brown curls ran up to us with open arms. Her feet were bare and she wore a ragged dress that was covered in poorly sewn patches, but the bright smile on her face made one forget her distressed attire.

She wrapped herself around Helle's legs and snuggled her face into the young girl's lap. "Helle!"

"Agatha!" Helle yelped as she wrapped her arms around the girl. "What are you doing here?"

Agatha raised her head and smiled up at Helle. "I wanted to come find you!"

"You shouldn't leave the house without me," Helle scolded her.

Agatha lowered her gaze to the ground and bit her lower, quivering lip. "I'm sorry. . .I just wanted to see you. . ."

Spiros handed his reins to Xander and walked over to the pair. He knelt in front of the pair and smiled at Agatha. "My name is Spiros. What's yours?"

The smile returned to Agatha's face. "It's Agatha!" She tilted her head to one side and studied him. "You look funny with your hand like that."

I followed her gaze and noticed Spiros lay his hand on his hip near where a hilt would be if he wore his sword. Spiros chuckled and rubbed the top of her hand with his hand. "You are very astute, Agatha."

She laughed and brushed away his hand. "You even talk funny."

"Would you like a treat?" he asked her.

Her eyes widened as did her smile. "Really?" She looked up at Helle. "Can I really have a treat?"

Helle bit her lower lip and her eyes flickered to Spiros. "I'm not sure. . ."

Spiros slipped his hand into his coat and drew out a small leather pouch held shut by strings. He pulled the strings apart and the mouth fell open to reveal dried berries that resembled raspberries, but they were as black as night.

Agatha's eyes widened as she stepped close to Spiros. "What are they?"

"A rare berry that I dried myself," he told her. "They are as sweet as sugar, but make you grow big and strong."

Agatha looked up at Helle and quivered her lower lip. "Please can I have one? Please?"

Helle sighed, but a smile teased the corners of her lips as she nodded. "You may."

The little girl squealed and clapped her hands as Spiros held the bag out to her. She took a small handful and popped a half dozen into her mouth. Her eyes bulged out of her head before she danced from foot to foot.

"They're so sweet!" she squealed.

Spiros chuckled as he shut the bag and tucked it back into his coat. "I did warn you," he scolded her as he stood.

Helle set her hands on Agatha's shoulders and turned the girl to face Spiros. "What do you say to the nice man?"

Agatha grinned and showed off her black-stained teeth. "Thank you!"

Spiros bowed his head. "You are quite welcome."

"Shall we finish off that wonderful dance with a drink inside?" Tillit offered.

Helle's smile fell from her lips and she shook her head. "We really should be going."

Agatha stopped her twitching and her face fell as she tilted her head back to look up at her guardian. "Do we have to?"

Helle nodded. "Yes. It's nearly dark and you still haven't had your supper." She turned them away, but paused and glanced over her shoulder at us. "Thank you-" her eyes flickered to Spiros, "-all of you, for your help today."

Spiros took a step toward her. "Might we see you tomorrow? We would be grateful for a local guide." Tillit wrinkled his piggish nose, but said nothing.

Helle shook her head. "I'm sure I wouldn't be very useful to you."

Agatha frowned up at Helle. "But you know so much about the lake! You could show them everything!"

MYTHS BEYOND DRAGONS

Xander arched an eyebrow at our new friend. "Is this true?"

Helle winced and turned her face away from us. "I'm afraid Agatha sometimes exaggerates, but thank you for your help again." She grasped one of Agatha's hands and hurried off down the darkening street.

"Well, if we're done with that let's get inside and I can treat you to my famous Twin Lakes Trout stew," Tillit spoke up.

He strode into the stables with Darda and Xander close behind him. I made to follow, but stopped when I noticed our group fell one short, and looked behind me. Spiros stood outside in the middle of the street and stared softly in the direction Helle and Agatha had gone. I walked up to him and noticed his gaze lay specifically on the tiny window through which I could see the figures of Helle and her young charge.

A sly grin slipped onto my lips as I tapped on the top of his shoulder. Spiros started at my touch and whirled around so fast he nearly knocked his elbow into my face. He reached for his waist where his sword usually lay.

I held up my hands and grinned at his serious face. "Easy there, lover boy. It's just me."

Spiros relaxed and resumed his forlorn staring. "Is it so obvious?"

I snorted. "If it was more obvious you'd be wearing a sign."

"She is quite beautiful, isn't she?" he mused.

I nodded. "Yep, and probably too good for you." He pursed his lips and his face fell a little. I sighed and set a hand on his shoulder. "I'm sure you'll see her again. No self-respecting woman would let you get away."

Spiros smiled and turned to me. "Thank you, Miriam."

I arched an eyebrow. "For what?"

He winked at me. "For speaking the truth in your heart."

Xander stepped out of the stables and his eyes fell on us. "Is something the matter?" he wondered.

"Nothing at all, Nester," Spiros called back as he strode toward our dragon lord. He paused by Xander's side and set a hand on his shoulder before he glanced back at me. "Though I feel I need to remind you that you have an excellent mate."

Spiros slipped inside and I joined Xander in front of the open door. He arched an eyebrow as he studied me. "Has something happened?"

I smiled and shook my head. "Nope, just a little falling in love."

I slipped inside and Xander followed. Our beasts lay contentedly atop fresh hay in their stalls and chewed on buckets of grain. Tillit led us into the adjoining house that proved to be as spectacularly large as the stables, and better furnished. The deep building had a single hall that followed the stable wall. On the opposite passage wall were doors to rooms. The stairs were situated in the front hall.

Oil lamps hung from those same walls and illuminated the comfortable space. Large rugs covered the wood-plank floor and the walls were whitened to perfection. Paintings and tapestries decorated the halls. Thick wood furniture such as a miscellaneous chair or a buffet finished off the space.

Tillit spun around to face us and grinned. "Welcome to my humble abode."

CHAPTER 15

Spiros swept his eyes over the area and whistled. "I had forgotten how long your family has prospered."

Tillit bowed his head to Xander. "We've had the honor of some wonderful patronage, but-" he straightened and gestured to the hall, "-let me feed you and then I can show you your rooms."

The sus led us down the hall to the first entrance which turned out to be a pair of double doors. Tillit opened them and revealed a long dining hall with a narrow table that seated ten. The table was already set with bowls of fresh fruit and a few plates of cold meat.

"It's not much, but help yourself," he offered.

"Were you expecting company?" I asked him as I took a seat beside Xander near the head of the table.

Tillit chuckled as he took the head seat. "No, but I have a healthy appetite, so I always give instructions for my cook to fix me up a large supper before she goes home."

I grabbed a fruit that resembled an apple and bit into it before I turned my attention to Xander. "So what are we doing first tomorrow?"

"We will see what you might find in reading the water," he told me as he snacked on some meat.

Tillit set his pudgy arms on the table and leaned close to us with an arched eyebrow. "Reading the water? What's that about?"

I turned and grinned at him. "My mom taught me how to see anything in the water just by touching it. I can even see stuff that's happening in the creeks and streams that feed something like the lake."

He whistled. "Impressive. You'd be invaluable to a fisherman, but how's this going to help you find a god, and what god are you looking for?"

Xander shook his head. "We do not know. The librarian of the Mallus Library could give us no details in that regard."

Tillit arched an eyebrow. "*The* Mallus Library?"

"The one and only," I confirmed.

He squinted his eyes and rubbed his chin. "What I wouldn't do for an hour among those books. I've heard stories about a collection of books that depict ancient trade routes that would make someone pretty wealthy."

"Wealth will not matter if we do not return the gods to their realm," Xander countered with a shake of his head. "That is why we will deal with the god first, and then handle the question of territory second." He glanced at me. "We might use one of the old docks far away from the city. That would be the safest in case something should go awry."

"I do not believe that will work," Spiros spoke up as he drew the Zoi map from inside his coat. He unfolded it on the table and swept his hand over the lake area, dragging forth a clear image of the Twin Lakes that hovered a foot above the table.

MYTHS BEYOND DRAGONS

Tillit tilted back his head and gaped at the image. "By all the gods. . ." he whispered.

Spiros used his free hand to point at the southern shoreline of the lake. The coastline was stacked with rocks that created a rugged dike to back the water. The remnants of many docks lined that shore, but most had either already fallen into the lake or looked like they were about to.

"Since the fisherman learned how to use the wind they have abandoned the docks along the dike," Spiros explained. "Without their constant care the docks have quickly succumbed to the winds and become unusable."

Tillit stood and leaned over the table so he could wave his hand through the image. The image blurred a little like a reception interruption, but otherwise was picture-perfect. He glanced at Spiros. "How are you doing this?"

Spiros grinned. "Has the great and knowledgeable Tillit never heard of the Zoi map?"

Tillit arched an eyebrow as he glanced back at the floating image. "I have, but this is beyond what I imagined it could do."

Xander leaned back and pursed his lips as he studied the image. "I see what you mean, Spiros. That means we must find a boat to rent. I will not risk the lives of my citizens should the god choose to show himself to be as dangerous as the librarian warned."

Tillit grinned. "Funny you should say that. I happen to have a boat wasting away its time on one of the docks."

"Yes, but-" he tapped his pudgy fingers against the map and frowned when an image appeared and disappeared as soon as it popped up, "-I would dearly love to know how this map works."

Xander rubbed his chin, and finally nodded. "That would not be a bad idea, to have one more user of the map. Should Spiros or I need to fly, you will be the keeper, Tillit."

Tillit bowed his head. "I would be delighted, My Lord."

"There is also something on which I wish to have your opinion," Xander added as he stood and walked over to our huddled supply bags. He rummaged around in mine until he drew out the small box that contained the bell. Xander returned to the table and set the box before Tillit.

The sus opened the lid and arched an eyebrow before he looked up at Xander. "What's this?"

"Our weapon against the gods," Xander explained as he resumed his seat. "The librarian gifted the bell to us so that we may send the gods back to their own domain."

Tillit slipped both hands beneath the bell and lifted it out. He turned it over in his hands and furrowed his brow. "How strange. It has a silver covering, but the rest of it is made of iron. The handle looks like it's made out of lefkankatha."

I blinked at him. "Made from what again?"

"In the common tongue lefkankatha means 'hawthorn,'" Xander explained to me.

"In ancient tales in both worlds the tree is known for its purifying qualities," Darda spoke up.

Tillit looked inside the small dome and arched an eyebrow. "There seems to be writing along the inside edge."

"Can you read it?" Xander asked him.

Tillit lowered the bell and frowned at him. "My Lord, there is not a language in this world Tillit cannot read." He cleared his throat and resumed his perusing of the letters. "It says 'Here you hold the Theos Chime.'"

"God bell," Xander translated for me.

"Then it continues with 'Ring Me Twice, Ring Me True, Ring the Gods, Ring the Two.'" Tillit glanced at the box before he turned his attention to Xander. "I hope you have another bell."

Xander shook his head. "No, but the rhyme does refer to ringing the bell twice. That may be the same 'two' referred to at the end of the rhyme."

MYTHS BEYOND DRAGONS

Tillit grabbed the wooden handle and gave the bell a swing to his right. The ball inside the dome hit the interior walls and made a hard clanking sound. He wrinkled his piggish nose and set the bell back in its case. "Not much of a bell."

"The rhyme did say something about ringing true," I teased.

He turned his nose up, but his eyes twinkled. "You hurt me, Miriam. Tillit is as true as his word."

"And as solid as your pocketbook," Spiros chimed in.

Tillit snorted as he handed the box back to Xander. "As the old saying goes: a sus must make a living, and a living is what makes a sus."

"And we should retire," Darda chimed in as she stood and took the bell box from Xander. Her eyes fell on me as she passed by to our bags. "Miriam looks exhausted, and I fear the water reading tomorrow will not do her any good."

Xander stood and nodded. "You are right, and the rough seas will not help us. Let us retire and rejoin early in the morning."

We finished our eating and Tillit led us to our upstairs rooms. They were furnished with the same luxurious trappings as the downstairs, but with the addition of thick-posted beds and dressers for our few clothes. The bell in its box was placed atop the dresser.

Xander and I received the bedroom at the front so that we had a window onto the main street. I opened one of the heavy wooden shutters and the window pane, and leaned on the large sill. The night was cool and calm, and the sweet scent of the lake wafted through the street and filled the city with an aroma of calm.

Xander came up behind me and wrapped his arms around my chest. I glanced up at his face and saw his eyes lay on the stars that twinkled above us. "Penny for your thoughts?" I whispered.

He looked down and arched an eyebrow. "What an unusual saying."

I shrugged. "I guess, but what are you thinking?"

Xander sighed and leaned his chin on my shoulder. "I was thinking that facing this god will be a greater challenge than any we faced before merely because we know nothing about him."

"Or her," I added.

He chuckled. "Or her, though I would prefer to face the wrath of a god than a goddess."

I shuddered. "I hope it doesn't come to wrath, but I guess we have to expect that, don't we?"

He pursed his lips and nodded. "Yes. We are a threat to their existence on this plain."

I looked down at the sill and bit my lower lip. "You know, after seeing where they came from I can't really blame them for wanting to stay here. I think I'd stay here, even if I *did* know I was causing chaos."

Xander snuggled me close against his chest and sighed. "It is their fate to live in that world, and we in ours."

I glanced up at him. "But I'm from another world."

"Is your presence destroying this one?" he countered.

My shoulders slumped and I hung my head. "No. . ."

"Then for the good of all the innocents-for the good of Agatha, Helle, and the like-we must return them to their world," he insisted.

I nodded. "I know, but still. . ."

He grasped my hands and led me toward the bed. "Leave your doubts for tomorrow. The night is for rest."

I lay down beside him with one of his arms wrapped around my waist, but it was a long time before the buzzing thoughts in my brain allowed me to sleep.

CHAPTER 16

Daylight was still a young visitor to the city when Xander and I walked down the stairs. Well, I stumbled a little, and my eyes were heavy with sleep. I rubbed them and glared up at Xander.

"Do we really need to be up at the butt crack of dawn?" I growled at him.

He chuckled. "Your sayings are becoming more amusing by the day, but we are awake at this hour because the winds are at their lowest during the night and early morning. Setting off early will ensure our safety."

Darda met us at the bottom of the stairs and smiled at me. "I hope you slept well."

"Too well. . ." I mumbled as we followed Xander down the hall.

We reached the open doorway that led into the dining room and paused. The fruit bowls had been replenished and fresh plates of ham, eggs, and bacon sat beside them.

Tillit sat at the head of the table with the Zoi map spread out in front of him. He eagerly pressed the fingers of one hand on every point of the map while his free right hand wrote down notes on a paper.

Beside him in the right-hand chair was the slumped figure of Spiros. The captain of the Alexandrian guards had his arms on the table and his forehead lay atop them. His regular breathing told us he was still in blissful dream land. I envied him.

Tillit noticed us and jumped to his feet. "My friends!"

His booming voice startled Spiros who's head shot up, revealing black pouches beneath his eyes. He whipped his head to and fro before his gaze settled on us. His face fell and he slumped down in his chair.

Xander smiled as he took the seat opposite his old friend. "Have you been here long?"

Spiros ran a hand through his short, frenzied hair. "Only all night."

"Our Lord ordered that Tillit should learn the secrets of the Zoi map," Tillit reminded him as he resumed his seat.

Spiros glared at him. "But all in one night?"

Xander chuckled as he slid an empty plate before him and began to fill it. "At least we have our two odigos."

Tillit wrinkled his piggish nose and shook his head. "I can't do as well as the captain here. These-" he lifted his short, pudgy fingers and the images were all sucked back into the map, "-won't let me do much more than work a few areas at a time."

"I am sure it will help, nonetheless," Xander insisted as he passed an empty plate to me as I took the seat beside him. "Now we should eat and remove ourselves to the docks."

A woman appeared in the doorway. She was a middle-aged woman of ample stomach and chest, but with thick arms that showed a life of constant work. A white apron splattered with fresh grease stains hid most of the of

MYTHS BEYOND DRAGONS

the front of her simple sheep-skin dress. Her long gray hair was tied into a bundle that gave her a severe look, but the twinkle in her eyes bespoke mischief.

"Tillit, you have a young visitor," she called to our host.

Tillit arched an eyebrow as he slid the map to Spiros and stood. The captain took the hint and hurriedly rolled up the map before he tucked it into his lap. "What beautiful young woman is it this time, Mrs. Pachis?" the sus asked her.

The woman snorted. "This would be the *first* time, Tillit, and I'll have you know she's not your type."

He grinned. "I have many different types, Mrs. Pachis."

"Not this one." She stepped to one side and another figure bounced into view.

It was Agatha. The young girl had a bright smile on her face as she bowed her head to us. "Good-" In her enthusiasm she nearly toppled over, but Mrs. Pachis caught her by the collar and straightened her. "Good morning!" she finished without missing a beat.

We couldn't help but smile at her adorableness. Mrs. Pachis's sly eyes flickered to Tillit. "You were saying, Tillit?"

Tillit cleared his throat and puffed out his chest. "I was saying, Mrs. Pachis, that you should get a plate for our young visitor."

Agatha shook her head. "Oh no, I can't stay long, but I wanted to give the nice man something."

Spiros stood-a rejuvenated man at the appearance of the young girl-and walked around the table to her. He knelt in front of her and smiled. "Something for me?"

Agatha smiled and nodded. "Yes. It's this-" She rifled through the single pocket on her tattered dress and drew out a small slip of folded paper that she held out to Spiros. "It's our address. Helle didn't want me to give it to you, but I think it's because she doesn't know how to court someone."

Spiros took the paper and pocketed it. "Thank you. I'll keep it safe."

Agatha stepped back and waved to us. "Bye!"

The bundle of energy spirited herself from the house. Spiros stood and turned to find all of us around the table smiling slyly at him. He coughed into his fisted hand. "The paper may prove useful if we need her help, or the other way around."

I snorted. "Yeah, sure. 'Help.'"

Xander stood, leaving behind him an empty plate with a few meager crumbs. "The hour is getting late. We must be on the water before the wind comes."

Tillit leaned back in his chair and shook his head. "You don't have to worry too much about that. It hasn't been a week yet."

Xander turned to him and arched an eyebrow. "What do you mean?"

Tillit picked up an apple and munched on a piece as he spoke. "The winds haven't been as bad-"

"Tillit, mind your manners," Mrs. Pachis scolded him.

Tillit swallowed his food. "As I was saying, they're not as bad as they used to be, especially on the lakes. Have been for two months. Before that there were some days even the best fishermen couldn't lift anchor, but with the new boat design and the off days the catch is as good as it's ever been. Now the lakes have a bad day, and then it won't happen for another week."

"So the wind has a schedule now?" I guessed.

He nodded. "Yep. It'll hardly be a gust today."

"When is the next gale due?" Spiros wondered.

"The last one was yesterday, so another six days," he told him.

Xander remained standing as he pushed his plate away from him. "Still, we should start our search early in case we should find problems."

MYTHS BEYOND DRAGONS

Our small group sighed, but obeyed our resident dragon lord and rose from the table. We fetched our coats and Darda took the bell in its bag, and soon were walking down the gentle hill to the tall wall.

I sidled up to Tillit. "What design of boat do you have?" I asked him.

He sheepishly grinned. "I have the old boat design-it's a family heirloom-but this being an off day we shouldn't have any trouble getting where Xander wants to go."

"How far out *do* we want to go?" I asked Xander.

"The center of the lake should provide enough distance," he replied.

We passed through one of the openings in the wall and were met by a gentle breeze, as Tillit foretold. The early morning sun shimmered across the rippling surface of the water as it stretched into the distance for some ten miles. The steep, rough foothills of the Heavy Mountains rose up on our left and traveled around until the Chasma separated a large chunk at the opposite end. The low dike to our right ran along the southern border until it rose upward at the far end and reached the Chasma where a speck of a building could be seen atop its rocky height, even from this distance.

"How deep is this thing?" I asked our company.

Tillit shook his head. "Nobody knows, or rather, the only ones who used to know are gone."

"You mean the Mare fae?" I guessed.

He nodded. "Yep. My great-granddad used to tell me stories about them that he heard from his granddad, but nobody's seen them since before even his time. Legends say they used to be worshiped around here and it wold calm the waters, but a couple thousand years ago that stopped working, so the people around here thought they left and forgot about them."

I looked at the ground and furrowed my brow. "I wonder if fae can die. . ."

"Nothing exists forever," Xander reminded me.

"These gods seem to," I pointed out.

He pursed his lips and glanced ahead of us. "Nothing *of* our world exists forever."

We reached the sandy white beach that curved around that end of the lake. Across the sands stretched two dozen docks of various shapes, sizes, and ages. The oldest-which made up some six of the docks-were jaggedly hewn from large trees and lashed together with ancient ropes that would have made the Gordian Knot look like a simple double-knot. The other docks were newer and cleanly cut from the local pine. Their planks and posted were pinned together with large nails driven in from end to end. They reached twice the distance out into the lake than their older counterparts, reaching some fifty yards long.

Ships of various sizes lazily rocked on the surface beside the docks. Men unloaded cargo, fresh fish caught in the earlier morning hours, and loaded them into wooden crates that were exactly like those we'd seen at the stables lower on the mountain.

I could tell the difference between the older style and the newer. The newer boats were deeper, making them more difficult to overturn in a swell. They had more than one sail, and the sails were different sizes and could be used all at once or alone. Heavy rock anchors sat on the new docks or were set into the water so they didn't rock against the gentle tide as their fishy cargo was unloaded.

Beyond the commercial and recreational docks and situated close to the tall, steep mountains were other piers. The ships docked along those planks were larger with two hundred feet of body and some with three masts. Their hulls were painted green with blue stripes, and the flag of Alexandria flew atop their crow's nests. Sailors in dark blue uniforms loaded provisions while others cleaned the open portals where I could see the mouths of cannons behind them.

MYTHS BEYOND DRAGONS

I glanced at my dragon lord, but nodded at the large ships. "Are those yours?"

He nodded. "Yes. Since aerial combat is impossible on the lakes Psychi must have a standing navy."

Tillit led us onto one of the older, shorter docks and up to a boat some thirty feet long with a single large sail. The boat wasn't so deep in the water and rocked to and fro in the gentle breeze. There were seats to accommodate all of us, with one at the stern, two in the middle and two tight spots at the bow. On the starboard side of the bow which faced us was written the name *Sweet Sus*.

Tillit stopped beside the ship and turned to us with a grin. "A beauty, isn't she?"

Spiros leaned over and studied the interior. A small pool of water sat on the bottom. "But is she seaworthy, captain?"

"As seaworthy as any," Tillit insisted.

Darda turned up her nose and snorted. "As any rock?"

The corners of Xander's mouth twitched as he stepped into the boat. The vessel rocked side-to-side, but remained afloat and no more water appeared on the bottom. "She appears sturdy, and we only have a short distance to travel."

Tillit puffed out his chest and grinned. "You heard your lord. Hop in."

While my companions stepped one-by-one into the boat I nodded at the name etched on the front. "Does that mean anything?"

Tillit followed my gaze and nodded. "Yep. My great-great-granddad named it after my great-great-grand-mum. Sweet in nature and Sweet in name."

Xander held his arms out to me. "We should be off."

I sighed, but took his offered hands and let him pull me into the boat so we could take the bow seats. "You know, you could enjoy the view once in a while," I told him.

He looked to his left and gazed out with pursed lips on the wide expanse of water. "When our mission is complete, but no sooner."

Tillit untied the boat and climbed into the vessel. The rigging for the sail stretched back to the rudder where Tillit took a seat. He wrapped the ropes around one hand and grabbed the rudder with the other. "Cast off, Skipper Spiros!"

"Aye, aye!" Spiros agreed as he set the bottom of one foot against the planks of the dock.

He gave a mighty push and sent us floating away from the birth. Tillit opened the sail and turned it with the ropes to catch the breeze. The wind filled the cloth and pulled us out into open waters. We moved at a good clip and soon left the shore far behind us.

I leaned over the starboard side and gazed into the water. The lake was a clear blue that allowed me to see down twenty feet. Small schools of fish scuttled past us or scattered completely. A few long tendrils of weeds peeked out from the dark depths and waved at us as we passed.

Beneath those signs of life lay an impenetrable darkness. It reminded me of all the forgotten back alleys and abandoned buildings of my old life where age had sunk into the boards, windows, and bricks. That sense of age warded off all but the most desperate or vile so that the alleys and buildings kept their secrets.

"You know, it's not too hard to imagine there's a god down there," I commented.

Xander glanced at Tillit. "This is far enough." The sus nodded and folded the sail so that we slowed and drifted along.

Xander returned his attention to me and nodded. I returned the gesture and rolled up my sleeve. Everyone tensed as I reached down. Darda clutched the bag with the bell to her chest.

MYTHS BEYOND DRAGONS

My hand was an inch from the water when a loud horn echoed across the lake. I froze and looked up at my companions. They all looked toward the Chasma.

"What's that?" I asked them.

Xander's pursed lips tightened as he stood and gaze out on the gap. "The horn of the Chasma. Someone has violated my lands."

CHAPTER 17

"Then sit down, My Lord, and let's see what's to be done about it," Tillit called out as he opened the sail.

The wind caught us immediately and propelled us forward. Xander was caught off-balance and toppled backward into the waiting arms of Darda and Spiros.

Darda whipped her head over her shoulder and glared at Tillit. "You fool! You could have thrown His Lordship overboard!"

Tillit chuckled. "His Lordship would never have missed this chase for all the world."

Darda rolled her eyes as Spiros steadied Xander. Xander stumbled back to the bow and plopped down in the seat beside me.

"So this horn warns everyone that the realm's being invaded?" I guessed.

He nodded. "Yes. Though the two realms had an accord, there was still distrust so each side placed their own warning machine atop the fortress to warn their people should the other realm betray them. The Black realm has a large gong, and my realm has a horn."

We were over three-quarters the way across the lake when Spiros shot up. "Stop the boat!" he commanded.

Tillit loosened his grip on the sail rope and frowned. The ship floated to a near stop and a good three miles lay between the Chasma and our position. "Why? We can't float there from this far away."

"When the horn is blown the orders are to fire on all approaching ships," Spiros told him.

I arched an eyebrow. "Fire with what?"

"The fire cannons," Xander spoke up as he looked gravely at the Chasma. "In the initial treaty, my ancestors built the Omonoia while Herod's family provided the defense, should either side break the concord. That defense is a set of six enchanted cannons, three facing either lake. They are capable of firing across half the water on either side."

Tillit wrinkled his piggish nose. "I've never heard of these cannons."

"Herod's ancestors were as cautious as he so that the secret of the cannons has remained with the two lordly houses and those charged with manning the fortress," Xander explained.

"But hasn't the fortress been empty for a while?" I reminded him.

He nodded. "Yes. When the fortress was abandoned five hundred years ago the cannons were hidden within its very walls. We cannot be completely sure they have been recovered, but Spiros is right that we should expect them to be at the ready."

"The last message that was received informed us the guards were making ready to excavate the cannons," Spiros told us.

"Then we must assume they have them at the ready," Xander replied.

"So how exactly do these magical cannons work?" I wondered.

"They need only a little ash tucked into their bore, or belly, and the fuse to be lit, and then they fire." He stepped closer to the bow and squinted at the Omonoia. "Though the muzzle is only six inches wide, the ball that is pushed forward grows to some three feet in diameter."

I winced. "That'd be hard to dodge."

"It is nearly impossible because the fireball is capable of changing course to match any target which lies on one half of the lake," he told me.

"So what do we do? Just sit here until we're sure it's safe?" I asked him.

He shook his head. "No. We must find a way to land and see what is the matter." He clenched his teeth and punched his hand into his other palm. "But for a light or a mirror, we might signal to them."

"Then I might have the solution," Spiros spoke up as he held his hand out to Xander. "If you would be so kind as to let me borrow Bucephalus." Xander arched his eyebrow, but stooped and drew the magnificent sword, protected inside its sheath, from his bag.

Darda watched them pass the weapon and frowned. "I do not believe wielding a weapon will help our standing with Omonoia."

Spiros smiled as he moved to the bow of the ship and sat on the tip so his legs dangled over. "The message this weapon will send will be a slightly different one," he returned as he lay the sword across his legs.

Spiros cradled either end of the sword in his open palms and tilted the weapon. The bright sun reflected off the shiny blade and, with each tiny movement, he created a flicker of light. Spiros rocked the weapon back and forth, gently and in different rhythms.

MYTHS BEYOND DRAGONS

My eyes widened. "Is that Morse code?"

He continued to stare straight ahead as he shook his head. "I do not know this 'Morse' you speak of, but I am sending a code."

A smile slipped onto Xander's lips. "You are using the ancient fire signals, but with light."

Spiros nodded. "That I am."

I slyly grinned and poked the back of his shoulder. "We'll have to tell Helle how you saved the day."

Spiros kept up his light communication for a few minutes before he stopped and shook his head. "It is no good. They have not replied."

"We're too far away," Tillit spoke up as he nodded at the rough surface around us. The light reflected off the white waves like the sword. "They probably think your sword talk is just another wave."

Xander pursed his lips and squinted at the far-off fortress. "If only we could see the walls."

A thought hit me and I snapped my fingers. "The map!"

Xander's eyes widened. "Of course!" He looked to Spiros, but the captain had already set aside Bucephalus and pulled out the Zoi map. He turned around and spread half of it open, the half that showed the lake. A simple flick of his fingers and the image of the Chasma appeared.

Xander and I scooted closer to the floating image. "We cannot see the Black side, but my realm is perfectly clear," he commented as he swept his gaze over the rocky fortress.

The Omonoia Fortress was built of rock fitted perfectly together. Its walls stood some thirty feet high and the structure stretched two hundred feet across an artificial flat spot on the southern side of the Chasma. There were three rows of windows along the long wall with the lowest only a foot above the ground, but they were all sealed with heavy wooden shutters.

111

"So what are we looking for?" I asked him.

Xander nodded at the lowest row of windows. "Those are where the cannons are hidden. Protocol demands that should a threat arise those are to be opened and the mouths of the cannons pushed forward so they stand even with the wall."

Spiros pursed his lips as he studied the map. "They are closed, but if the danger lies on the eastern lake they might have failed to follow protocol."

Xander shook his head. "We have no choice. Duty demands we learn the reason for the horn, so we must move closer so that they might see your signaling and give a response." He glanced over his shoulder at the sus at the helm. "Open the sail and draw us closer."

Tillit saluted him and drew the sail open. "Aye aye, captain!"

The wind flew across the lake, and Spiros continued sending his message. We tensed as we crossed the mile threshold without a reply.

"At what point do we start panicking?" I spoke up.

The Chasma with its sheer walls and rocky base loomed in front of us. I could make out a narrow set of stairs carved from the rocks that wound its way from the water up to the fortress.

Darda pursed her lips as she glanced at Xander. "My Lord. . ."

Xander's attentive eyes remained focused on the fortress. They widened, and he pointed at the top row of windows. "There!"

I followed his finger and noticed that a pair of shutters in front of one of the windows had been removed. A figure stood there with a large mirror and flashed a message back at us.

"What are they saying?" I asked my companions.

"They will grant us leave to land," Darda told me. Xander glanced at her and arched an eyebrow. She smiled.

MYTHS BEYOND DRAGONS

"At one point your mother was most adamant that we both learn the military signals."

Spiros stopped his signaling and pointed at the bottom of the stairs. A small flat piece of ground with an old dock stood there. "Land there."

Tillit guided our boat to the left side of the dock. On the opposite side was anchored a larger ship with the crest of Xander's family on both sides of the bow.

Xander turned to all of us. "I would ask you do not reveal my identity."

I frowned. "Why not? And why wouldn't they recognize you?"

"I would rather not alert the two battling factions of the Black realm that I am present, and not all who are under my command know me," Xander explained.

We had only climbed out of the boat when we saw a dozen dragon men in march down the steps in single file. They each held the strange sickle-staff native to the area, and when we met them on the flat land they pointed the weapons at us.

It wasn't quite the welcome I'd been hoping for.

CHAPTER 18

One of them stepped forward, an officer who wore a small pani horn on the front of his helmet. "You are all under arrest."

Tillit glanced at Spiros. "What exactly did you tell them?"

Spiros stepped forward and straightened to his full height. "There must be a mistranslation in my message. I am Spiros, captain of-"

"There is no mistranslation," the officer interrupted as his men surrounded us with their sharp staffs. "But we find it hard to believe the captain of Alexandria would be found here so soon after the horn is blown. What business brought you here?"

Xander's eyes flickered to him, so Spiros shook his head. "That is confidential, but you may be assured it is business of the crown that brings me here."

The officer shook his head. "That's not good enough."

I leaned toward Xander and gave him a soft nudge. His eyes flickered to me and I jerked my head toward the water behind us. All I had to do was twitch my fingers and we'd be out of this mess, but he shook his head.

The officer swept his gaze over the rest of our group. "This is a rather unusual group for a captain of Alexandria to travel with." His eyes fell on Xander and he marched up to him. "What is your name?"

"Nester," Xander replied.

"Occupation?"

"A humble traveler."

The officer pursed his lips. "What business do you have on these lakes?"

Xander nodded at Spiros. "We follow our leader."

I stifled a snort, but that caught the attention of our interrogator. He stepped up to me and frowned. "What lies will you tell me, human?"

"None, if you don't ask my any questions," I quipped.

The officer's lips curled back in a snarl. He spun around and marched outside the ring of weapons before he paused and looked over his shoulder at us. "We'll interrogate you in the fortress, but if you try anything on the way up my men won't hesitate to throw you into the water. Now march."

So we found our hands tied behind our backs and separated by the guards. One of the men took Bucephalus from Spiros and handed it to their leader who looked it over before he raised his gaze to the captain.

"This is a rather unusual sword for a spy," he commented.

Spiros smiled. "It is for a spy, but we are not spies."

The officer tucked the sheath into his belt and jerked his head toward the stairs. "That will be for the captain to decide."

The soldiers marched us up the narrow steps in single file. Spiros was the first of our group followed by Xander, me, Darda, and Tillit.

"This is a first. Captured by our own allies. . ." I muttered.

"Quiet back there!" the officer shouted.

I stuck my tongue out at him. The guard behind me knocked the blunt end of his staff against my left side. "No disrespect to our officer!"

I didn't have an opportunity to argue as his hard smack against my back had all the strength of his dragon lineage behind it while my back had all the weakness of my human-fae self. The result was that I lost my balance in the worst direction, my right, where the steep drop came with a sudden stop atop the jagged rocks that surrounded the base of the Chasma.

I stumbled over my own feet as I tried to gain a literal foothold on the barren path. One of my feet stepped out into the nothingness and I felt myself tip toward the chasm.

Xander spun around and tried to help me, but the guard in front of me blocked his path. "Miriam!"

I screamed as I tipped over into the drop. My guard tried to catch me, but his hand missed my arm as I twisted into my fall. I plunged head-first down the steep cliff and watched the look of horror on my friends' faces while Xander wrestled with all of the guards to follow me, and they were losing.

"Miriam!" Darda cried as Tillit, Spiros and she rushed to the edge to watch my end.

The rock wall flew past me with my body just barely missing some of the outcroppings. The wind whipped my hair into my face. I sputtered some strands out of my mouth and I looked below me. The water came up fast. Two seconds and I'd be a red stain on the stones.

Fortunately, I wasn't some wimpy damsel in distress. I focused my eyes on the water that surrounded those deadly rocks. From the depths of those deadly deeps drew a pair of water dragons, the same pair I'd made appear at the Island of Red Fire. They twisted around one another and caught me between their joined bodies.

I looked up at them and grinned. "Thanks, guys." Their bright blue-green eyes twinkled in reply. One of them snapped its jaws through my bound hands, and the ropes fell apart.

I was rubbing my wrists when I heard shouts above us and looked up at the stone stairway. The guards had Xander pinned to the wall while the others gaped at me far below them. My eyes flickered to my wet pets and I jerked my head up at the group.

The water dragons stretched upward, taking me with them until we came to a stop five feet higher on the stone steps than the guards and my friends. I stepped off while my dragons snarled at the guards.

Their leader pointed his staff at my beasts, but looked to me with narrowed eyes. "What witchery is this?"

"It's no witchery!" Xander spoke up from his pinned position. His eyes met mine and there was a warning in them. "She has been blessed by the Mare fae of the lakes."

The leader scoffed. "Everyone knows there are no Mare fae in the lakes."

I crossed my arms over my chest and jerked my head to my left where my dragons stood glaring at the guards. For their part they pressed themselves against the cliff wall far away from my beasts, nearly suffocating my friends. "So how do you explain them?"

The pointy-helmeted fellow pursed his lips at me. "Being blessed by any fae doesn't disprove that you are spies, and if you wish to free your friends you will come with us."

I nodded at my former guard who quaked more than the rest. "Fine, but tell him not to push me around, or these babies-" I gestured to my dragons who snapped their jaws at the guards, making some of them yelp, "-will teach you guys how to behave."

The leader half-turned to his subordinate. "You will refrain from mistreating the prisoners, do you understand?" The guard fervently nodded his head. If he'd tried any harder he would have lost it where I fell.

I dropped my hand and the dragons disappeared into the water far below us. The leader walked up to me and jerked his head up the steps. "After you."

I smiled and nodded. "My pleasure."

I led the way up the cliff steps, but it was a bittersweet victory with my friends still tucked between the guards. We climbed for another three hundred feet before the trail leveled out and widened. Five hundred feet in front of us stood the rectangular building known as Omonoia. A pair of metal doors on the ground floor faced us, and on each side stood another guard with his sickle staff. They tensed at our coming, and one of them banged his fist behind him on the door.

The leader of our guard group stopped us fifty feet from the door and raised his staff above his head. "Prasinos!" he called out.

"Ble!" one of the guards at the door called back, and both of them lowered their weapons.

A snort burst from Tillit's nostrils. "Green and blue? Those are you passwords? If we were spies this would be too easy to get into."

The guard leader glared at him, but didn't have time for a reply for the metal doors creaked open. A half dozen more guards stepped out, and at their head was a tall dragon man. He had the bearing of a lord, what with his stiff back and upturned nose. Atop his head and tucked beneath his pani-sporting helmet the man had a flaming crop of red hair, the perfect color to match his pursed lips and the anger in his eyes as he marched up to us.

MYTHS BEYOND DRAGONS

He glanced at the leader of the guards. "Who are these trespassers?"

The leader of our welcoming party shook his head. "We do not know, Captain Kokinos, but this dragon-" he nodded at Spiros, "-had this in his possession." He held out in both his hands the sheath of Bucephalus with the sword contained therein.

Captain Kokinos took the sheath and drew Bucephalus halfway out. The shimmering sword reflected his arched eyebrow before his eyes flickered up to Spiros. "Where did you get this?"

"From our lord himself, Xander," Spiros admitted.

"And you are-?" Kokinos persisted.

Spiros smiled and bowed low to him. "Captain Antonios Spiros, leader of the Alexandrian guard and counsel to Lord Xander Alexandros the VI."

I blinked at the captain. "Spiros isn't your first name?"

He straightened himself and shook his head. "No, merely a family name."

"Can you prove this illustrious name is yours?" Kokinos questioned him.

Spiros nodded at the sword. "That is some proof, for the sword you hold is Bucephalus, the white sword of the lake."

He snorted. "A sword can be stolen or forged. That does not prove you are not spies."

"If that were true then you would be the bigger fool for allowing us so close to the fortress," Spiros countered. The revelation made the captain grind his teeth together. "Fortunately, we are not spies. If my knowledge of the code is not proof enough-"

"It is not," he snapped.

"-than that sword-" Spiros nodded at Bucephalus as it lay in the captain's hand, "-is all I need to convince you I am Captain Spiros. You will find that it can cut through any metal you place before it."

Captain Kokinos pursed his lips before he half-turned away from us and jerked his head toward the open doors. "Follow me."

CHAPTER 19

We followed Kokinos inside the fortress. The interior was as bleak as the exterior with rough stone floors and walls. Torches lit the narrow hall that ran from end-to-end. A door on our left led down a flight of narrow, winding stone steps to I assumed the sub-floor. On our right were the stairs the led up to the second floor.

Kokinos led us up the right-hand stairs and to a narrow hall that ran along the center again. On either side were open spaces interrupted only by thick wooden support beams. Cots lined the walls, and a few soldiers relaxed on them. At the coming of their captain, however, all the leapt to their feet and stood at attention.

"As you were," Kokinos ordered them as he led us past his men to the back wall.

A door stood at the back wall, and it was through this that we entered a small room. There was a cot on either side and two desks in the middle. Only one bed had blankets, the bed on the left, while the other was dusted but empty. On either wall was a window, and both were opened to the opposing lakes. Sheets of metal had kept them closed, but now they leaned against their respective walls with the shutters opened above them.

Kokinos turned to our large group and glanced at our escort party. "Remain outside. I need only three men to manage them." The men nodded, and the needed number remained while the others stepped out and shut the door behind them.

Spiros swept his eyes around the room. "In your last dispatch I was informed the cannons would soon be put at the ready. Is that the case?"

The captain ignored the question as he set his hand on the sheath of Bucephalus and drew out the sword. The white blade shimmered like starlight even in the sunlit room. The captain glanced around before his eyes settled on one of the slim sheets of metal that had kept the windows shuttered. He walked over and stood before the metal before his eyes flickered to one of his subordinates.

"Hold that metal away from the wall," he ordered him.

The officer pulled the sheet away so the metal stood upright perpendicular to the wall. The captain raised the sword, and in one fell swoop he brought the blade down on the sheet. The metal parted like soft butter beneath the wicked blade of Bucephalus. The half not held by the subordinate clattered to the ground at the captain's feet.

The captain turned to us and frowned at Spiros. "It appears what you say is true, but how did you come to have this sword? Theft? Coercion?"

Spiros snorted. "Do you believe Lord Xander would merely hand over this sword to anyone who asked-" I had a hard time containing my snort, "-or that I could steal such a weapon from our lord? It was given to me as a signal to you that I am to be trusted."

MYTHS BEYOND DRAGONS

Captain Kokinos shook his head. "This sword only proves its own identity, not yours."

Spiros pursed his lips. "You are a difficult man to convince, Captain Kokinos, but I have other proof if someone would untie me."

The captain narrowed his eyes. "Why?"

"So I may unbutton my shirt," Spiros explained.

"You needn't be untied for that," Kokinos argued as he nodded at one of his men.

The guard stepped up to Spiros and opened his coat before he grasped the edges of his shirt. Spiros winced as the man parted his shirt, tearing the buttons off and revealing his bare chest. I gasped as I beheld a long, jagged scar that ran from his waist up his chest to his sternum. The wound was ancient, but even time couldn't heal the flesh that had been torn away by a sharp, merciless claw. The skin was a mix of gray and pink, and the flesh was bumpy where stitching had held the sides together.

Captain Kokinos's eyes widened before he whipped them up to Spiros's face. "The. . .the Mark of the Reod."

Spiros shook himself so his shirt fell back and hid the hideous scar. "I am glad you know of it, Captain, and trust you will now inform my companions and me the reason why you blew the horn."

Captain Kokinos swallowed the lump in his throat and nodded. "I-I must apologize, sir, for such precautions, but it is because of why we blew the horn that it was necessary to prove who you were."

"And that is-?" Spiros persisted.

The captain pointed at the right-hand window. "A ship approached the Chasma and violated our waters."

Spiros arched an eyebrow. "Your last report did not say you had blown the horn at each violation."

Kokinos shook his head. "No, because they were not *royal* ships."

Xander straightened and his eyebrows crashed down. "Philip himself has violated the realm?"

Kokinos looked to him and nodded. "That is what we believe. However, the boat quickly turned around and returned to the upper lake where it still resides near the Chasma."

Xander strode over to the window and looked out. I joined him and beheld the upper lake. It was about the same size and oval shape as the lower body of water, and at the far end was another city. However, the Heavy Mountains loomed up on our left and blanketed the area in its long shadow. I could make out an empty area devoid of buildings that was nestled against the foothills of those formidable mountains.

Xander looked down, and I followed his gaze to the waters below the Chasma. They were nearly as rocky as those on the lower lake side, but a gentle tide of countless years had worn their tops away to smooth platforms.

The largest of the rocks was twenty feet square and stood a hundred feet off the Chasma. A large two-mast ship was anchored along its farthest side from where we stood. The sails and body were painted black, but a crest stood out at the bow. I could make out a black wing over a white circle.

Xander pursed his lips. "That is indeed the crest of the Black dragon." He half-turned to Kokinos. "What actions have you taken against the ship?"

Kokinos shook his head. "Nothing but sound the horn."

Xander turned his attention to Spiros. "We must meet him, if Philip is indeed aboard that ship."

Spiros nodded and smiled at Kokinos. "If you would be so kind as to untie us we will meet the prince on behalf of our lord."

My friends were duly untied and Bucephalus returned to Spiros. We were escorted by the captain himself out of the fortress. Xander turned to the right side of the cliff, and we followed. A flight of stone steps that was the mirror image of those on Xander's side was revealed to us, though there was evidence of disrepair in the cracked steps and broken-off corners.

The captain came up behind us and shook his head. "The way down this side of the Chasma is much too dangerous. Though the winds are calm they are unpredictable around these rocks, so I would recommend you take the other route and go to your ship."

"How come this one's so much worse?" I asked him.

He nodded at the gray city in the distance. "The family of Herod abandoned the fortress and sought that no one else should be able to use the steps, so they left them to the elements."

Xander glanced at me. "Do you believe you are able to call upon the 'blessing' of the Mare fae in order that we may reach the ship?"

I grinned. "I can ask."

I walked to the edge and knelt close to the steep drop. The waters far below me splashed unceasingly against the stones in a never-ending attempt to wear away the Chasma. I focused my gaze on those rough seas. The water bubbled and from the depths rose five dragons that were half the size of my largest. They stretched their long bodies upward until they reached me where the group slipped around me like puppies. I smiled and petted them.

Captain Kokinos gaped at the water dragons. "By all the gods..."

I shook my head. "No, just a fae. Anyway, let's go."

Four of my little dragons swooped past me and slipped between the legs of my companions. Darda yelped and clutched onto the neck just below the head as she was swept off her feet and drawn over the edge. Xander and Spiros majestically sat tall on their beasts as they followed my terrified handmaiden over the cliff.

Seeing the fate of the others, Tillit scuttled backwards and turned to flee. "I'd rather take my-" The dragon slipped between his legs, but the wrong direction so that he was mounted backwards. He squealed and wrapped himself around the dragon's body as he was carried into the air.

The last dragon picked me up and together with my friends we descended in a diagonal line toward the awaiting ship.

CHAPTER 20

A sailor stood watch in the bird's nest of the largest of the two masts, and at our coming he raised a cry. More sailors rushed out of the hatch in the middle of the deck with swords tucked into their belts. They unsheathed their weapons and crowded the part of the deck closest to us. Even from a great distance I could see some of their eyes widen at our mode of transportation.

At the rear of the ship was a cabin. The door opened and out stepped a handsome but pale young man of twenty. He had jet-black hair that was slicked back like a streak. His attire consisted of matching black pants and a blouse shirt. A black overcoat covered most of him and reached to the top of his black boots.

A smile slipped onto his pale lips as we approached. He motioned to his men who slipped their weapons back into their belts. Xander and I reached the rocky island first and my dragons set us down. Our friends followed behind us, and Spiros moved to the front of our small group.

"We come in peace!" he shouted.

The man in black walked down the plank with only two burly escorts behind him. He stopped five feet from our group and looked us over. "What a fascinating group you are." His attention fell on Spiros and the sheath on his hip. "That is a very unique-looking sword, Sir-?"

"Spiros of the Alexandrian guards," Spiros replied.

The man arched an eyebrow. "Though your name is well known to many, that is a very great sword for a mere captain to possess."

"You forgot to mention your name," I spoke up.

The stranger smiled and bowed his head to me. "You are quite right, Your Ladyship. I apologize for my rudeness to you, the guests in my realm." He bowed low to us. "I am Philip Keper, heir to the Black realm and current master of Zem."

"What business do you have violating the waters of the Green realm?" Spiros questioned him.

Philip held up his hand. "As honored as I am to meet the famous Spiros of Alexandria, I would rather speak with your lord himself." He turned to Xander and bowed his head. "Your Lordship."

Xander pursed his lips. "Then you know who I am?"

Philip raised his head and smiled. "Of course. Though I was a young lad the last time I saw you, your legendary good looks have not changed." His eyes flickered to me. "And this must be your Maiden. She is as beautiful as the rumors say, and I no longer doubt that the other rumors are true."

I arched an eyebrow. "What other rumors?"

Philip folded his arms across his chest and shrugged. "Merely that you hold the power of water in her hands, a strength great enough to subdue even a Red dragon lord."

"I believe you have violated my waters for more than to chat about rumors," Xander spoke up.

Philip sighed and nodded. "Yes. I apologize for my boorish behavior, but I thought a face-to-face meeting would be more preferable to a simple correspondence, and what better way to attract your attention than feign an invasion?"

"You could have written," I suggested.

He chuckled. "Writing would hardly have conveyed the severity of the issue. You see, I wish to make an alliance with you against my beautiful cousin Salome."

Xander shook his head. "I will not draw my own people into your family squabbles."

"Ah, but I believe my cousin intends to do just that, namely in attacking Omonoia," Philip revealed.

"What proof do you have that your cousin plots against the fortress?" Xander asked him.

Philip looked to his right at one of his men. The officer stepped forward and drew from inside his coat a small glass bottle with a cork at the top of its neck. Inside the bottle was a rolled up piece of paper. Philip took the bottle and tossed it at Xander who neatly caught it in one hand.

"Read it for yourself," Philip invited him.

I leaned against Xander's shoulder as he popped open the cork and tapped the paper onto his open palm. He tucked the bottle beneath his arm and unrolled the paper. A short message was written in an elegant, scrawling hand.

The stone building will be attacked by one of your own. Beware the other.

Xander frowned and looked up at Philip. "Where was this found?"

Philip nodded at the Chasma. "It was found floating in the Far, or Chasma, as you refer to the gap."

Xander narrowed his eyes. "On your side or mine?"

The young would-be lord smiled and shrugged. "My men graciously decided to do your side a favor and picked up that piece of trash. It was well they did for it has warned us of the impending attack on the fortress by my dear cousin."

Tillit glanced over Xander's other shoulder and wrinkled his nose. "It's a little vague. Are you sure it's meaning your cousin and not a wild herd of pani?"

Philip frowned and turned his nose up at Tillit. "A sus has no business in the affairs of dragons."

Tillit grinned. "You'd be surprised how the business of sus are the affairs of dragons."

"He is right," Xander spoke up as he rolled the paper up and slipped it back into the bottle. "This proves nothing against your cousin, and is certainly not proof enough for my realm to wage war against a part of your family." He plugged the cork back in the top and tossed the bottle back to our host.

Philip caught the bottle as his eyebrows crashed down. "You do realize that should I win this struggle against my cousin that your lack of faith in my word will be a great wound between our two houses."

Xander shook his head. "It is not your word I doubt, but your interpretation of the message. Bring me proof that Salome herself is involved and I will be persuaded to protect my realm against her."

Philip's frown deepened as he handed the bottle back to his man. "I see I cannot sway your mind, but I hope you will not come to regret your decision. Good day." He turned and strode back to his ship.

"Well, that could have gone better," Tillit quipped.

MYTHS BEYOND DRAGONS

I looked up at Xander. His lips were pursed as his eyes remained on the back of the young man as Philip walked up the plank and onto the ship. I tugged on his sleeve and lowered my voice to a whisper. "You okay?"

He shook his head. "There is a war brewing on the lakes, and I cannot see how I will be to keep my subjects safe from its effects."

"*You* don't have to do anything, but *we* are all going to save the day," I corrected him.

He glanced over his shoulder at all of our friends. Tillit puffed out his chest and grinned while the other two smiled and bowed their heads. A smile slipped onto his lips as he returned his attention to me. "I see what you mean, my Maiden."

I tapped the end of his nose. "*Miriam*."

"Miriam," he rephrased.

I clapped my hands and rubbed them together as I turned to my friends and lover. "Well, what's next on the trouble agenda?"

"Your water reading," Tillit spoke up as he dropped his ample stomach. "I'd like to see how this is done."

Darda pursed her lips. "I do not believe having Miriam read the water would be a wise course of action. We do not know if this god is benevolent or dangerous."

Xander looked out over the waters as Philip's ship pulled away from our little island. The black sails spread wide and drew the ship quickly across the lake toward the gray city. "If we rely on the words of the librarian it would be wise of us to expect danger."

"Then is there not some other way to draw the god from the water?" she persisted.

"Crates was pretty firm that Xander and I needed to do the work," I told her.

"But-"

Tillit set a hand on her shoulder and grinned at her. "With you at her side, my dear Darda, no god in the world would dare touch your mistress."

Darda shrugged off his hand, but a smile teased the corner of her lips. "We shall see."

Xander turned to us and nodded. "Yes. Let us return to our own realm."

CHAPTER 21

With the aid of my dragons I returned us the Omonoia. Captain Kokinos waited for us where we left him. The mouths of his men were agape, but his mouth was shut tight as he set his eyes on Spiros. "What news, Captain Spiros?"

"The vessel is owned by Philip Keper, but we do not expect him to violate our waters again," Spiros assured him.

Captain Kokinos's gaze flickered to Xander. "Your companion here seemed to hold his attention quite well."

Spiros smiled at Xander. "My companion has a way of inserting himself into conversations that do not concern him, but if other trouble will arise you may find us in Psychi. Good day."

We left the cold welcome of the stone fortress and returned to Tillit's ship. The wind was a little stronger, but a push from Spiros and Tillit guided us back out to the center of the lake. I leaned over the side and looked down into the dark water now marred by waves.

Xander set a hand on my shoulder. "If you have any qualms we might wait until tomorrow."

I smiled and shook my head. "I'm fine. Besides, I don't think another day is going to make the god any happier to see us, or hear what we have to say."

Darda patted the bag that held the bell box. "Or hear."

"Or hear," I agreed as I leaned over the edge of the boat. I took a deep breath and dipped my hand into the water.

The lake, being so deep, was cold as the waves gently lapped against my hand. I focused my mind on the little ripples that made up the current, and a thousand different pictures came to my mind. There were the fish that swam through abandoned nets and the turtles that coasted through the rocks that lined the shores.

A greater ripple, however, blotted out those gentle images and brought with it a cold wind. The image that ripple created in my mind was one of a pair of narrowed eyes surrounded by swirling droplets of water. Those eyes zeroed in on me and I felt a hot blast of anger sweep over me.

I gasped and started back, drawing my hand from the water and back to the real world. That world was much the same as a violent wind swept from the north and across the lake to where we floated. The sturdy ship rocked from side-to-side and the sails flapped in every direction.

The gale focused itself in a small wind devil that appeared north of our position and thirty feet off the starboard. The winds spun in a wild circle for a few tense moments before they exploded outward, rocking our ship like an eruption.

In place of the gale was a young man of fifteen. He had short white hair that remained still atop his head despite the wind that still circled his person. His clothes were a simple shirt and pants, and his feet were bare. The oddity of his attire was a cloak made from a ram skin that was draped across his thin shoulders. He floated twenty feet above the rough surface and stared down at us with the same eyes I'd seen in my water reading.

Xander rose to his feet and steadied himself amid the rocking as he faced the angry young man. "Who are you?" he shouted above the wind.

The young man ignored Xander's question as his gaze fell on me. "You have invaded my privacy, fae-child."

"And you've made me sea-sick," I quipped.

His pale eyebrows shot down. "You are not native to this area. Why are you here?"

I held up a hand. "In order for me to answer that question I have to ask: are you a god?"

The young man straightened and narrowed his eyes. "Do not speak so lightly of my personage."

I snorted. "Yep, he's a god. Nobody else could have that much ego."

Xander stepped in front of me so that he blocked the god's view of me. "By the command of the librarian and the people of this world we must ask you to leave and return to your own world," he commanded him.

He scoffed. "I care not for either party. My interest lies only in defending what is mine from the intrusions of your kind."

"And what exactly is yours?" Spiros spoke up.

The young god looked down his nose at the captain. "The lakes and all the lands that touch them."

"They are not yours, nor is anything else in this world," Xander argued.

"I grow tired of your foolish prattle, mortals." He waved his hand at us and stirred the winds to a rough gale. "Leave or I will shipwreck you."

I gripped the side of the boat as the wild waves rocked the vessel from side-to-side so harshly that she threatened to capsize. A heavy wave hit the side of the boat and drenched us with its cold water. I shook the droplets loose from my hair before I whipped my head to Xander. "I don't feel sorry for him anymore!"

He grinned. "Good, then let us send him back to his realm."

Xander grasped the side of the boat and used it as a crutch to stumble over to the bag. He drew out the box that held the bell and clutched it against his chest as the boat was rocked by another cold wave.

One look at the box made the god's eyes widen. He floated back a few feet and raised one arm in front of him. Even with the loud waves I could hear his strangled words. "The Theos Chime!"

Xander grasped the mast and stood as he tucked the box beneath his other arm. "Will you return to your own world, or must we send you there?"

The god's brow crashed down and he lowered both his arms to his sides. "So you mean to banish me? I shall not allow it! May you all sink to the bottom of my lake!"

Our foe snapped his fingers and the cyclone reappeared around him. He disappeared into the winds and the swirling cyclone spun toward us. The wind whipped at the sail and tore the thick canvas into strips. My hair and clothes slapped my face and body as half my body hung over the railing.

Tillit wrapped himself around the rudder and tried to keep the boat from turning sharply and capsizing. "Fly, anyone who can!" he shouted above the roaring winds.

Darda whipped her head up and glared at him. "You fool! It would be the death of us if we tried to take flight now! The wind would knock us into the water and the pain would be as though it was a wall of stone!"

"Hold on to the boat!" Xander shouted as he handed the box back to Darda.

MYTHS BEYOND DRAGONS

He grasped the sides of the ship and his wings sprouted from his back. So great and tall were they that they replaced the torn sail and then some. The wind filled his wings and shot us forward. The cyclone followed us as the winds beat at Xander's wings. It was like a game of cat and mouse where every move by the cat was mimicked by the mouse so that we kept an even distance from the cyclone.

Unfortunately, we weren't staying an even distance from the southern shoreline. The dike loomed up on us along with its large, sharp rocks that made up the base that was covered by water.

I tried to stand and stumbled toward Xander where I grabbed his shoulder and swung myself in front of him. My moves gave me a view of his face. I couldn't help but gasp when I saw his eyes. They were red and green. His face was contorted into pain and anger. I glanced at his hands. They were more claws than fingers, and dug so deep into the wood that splinters cut into his hands. Red blood dripped onto the floor boards and mixed with the water to create a sickening pinkish liquid.

Tillit grabbed the rudder and yanked it so we were pulled in the opposite direction, but for every foot in that direction the waves of the cyclone forced the entire boat starboard an equal distance so we still edged closer to the rocks.

"Steer us away!" Darda shouted at him.

"I can't!" Tillit replied.

Impact was inevitable. Spiros threw himself atop Darda and Tillit hugged the rudder. I wrapped my arms around Xander and focused my energy on the swirling waters around us. My dragons loomed up, but their bodies were washed to pieces by the raging storm. They couldn't save us as the starboard side of the ship bounced off its first rock.

A moment before our doom a dark shadow enveloped us.

CHAPTER 22

I felt a familiar sense of pressure around me, but Xander's warm body kept my mind from panicking. Like all horrors, the darkness ended and the way opened up to calm air and bright sunlight. It also opened up to a short drop.

Darda and I yelped as the ship sailed out of the darkness and dropped a feet to the hard ground, but even the muddy dirt didn't stop our fast sailing ship. We slid for ten feet before coming to a rest amid some grass. The vessel, battered and bruised, burst asunder and its planks scattered across the soft ground on which we found ourselves. I opened one squeezed eye and glanced around.

At our backs lay the woods of the pass, and in front of us stood one of the houses of the outpost managed by Kyrios. Beside and a little behind the home was parked a wagon filled with the familiar wooden crates I'd seen along the docks of Psychi. The house had a pair of storm cellar doors that both lay open, and a woman stood near the top facing us. Her eyes were wide and her mouth was agape.

"What's keeping you, woman?" a male voice snapped as the speaker's head appeared above ground.

The man froze when he saw us and his eyes bulged out of his head. His gaze moved past us. I twisted around and followed it. There, ten feet behind us us, swirled a dark portal.

A groan beside me reminded me I wasn't the only one to have the 'fun' time of going through the portal. Xander, with his wings once more hidden, lay slumped under the remains of the mast.

"Xander!" I shouted as I stumbled to my feet and started lifting bits of wood off him.

Spiros and Darda burst out from beneath a nearby pile of planks. Spiros's eyes fell on our dragon lord and widened before he hurried over to us. Darda soon joined, and in a moment we had the planks removed from Xander.

I knelt beside him and gave his shoulders a shake. "Xander! Xander, wake up!"

He stirred and his eyes fluttered open. His gaze settled on me and a teasing smile slipped onto his quivering lips as he spoke a few whispered words. "It is Nester, my dear Miriam."

I frowned at him. "It was almost pancake for you."

Spiros checked his body and pursed his lips. "You have a few bruised ribs."

Xander shook his head and sat up on his own power, though not without wincing. "I am-" Spiros stabbed a finger against Xander's side. Xander cried out and clutched his injured side.

"You were saying, My Lord?" Spiros asked him.

Xander's eyes flickered up and glared at him. "I was saying I am in need of a new captain of the guard."

A noise made us look to the back of the ruined ship. Tillit rose from his wrecked vessel with the remains of the rudder stick still in his hand. "One of these adventures will be the death of me," he commented as he stumbled through the planks. He swept his eyes over the ship and sadly shook his head. "I'm glad Grandpa isn't alive to see this. It'd kill him."

"My Lord?" a familiar voice called, forcing our attention toward the house. Kyrios hurried out of the cellar and over to us with two men behind him. They stopped at the start of the wrecked ship and he shook his head as he studied the ruination. "By all the gods, what has happened?"

I pointed up at the swirling darkness over our heads. "That happened."

Kyrios followed my finger and gaped at the portal. "*Another* portal?"

Xander frowned at his stable master. "What do you mean another portal?"

Kyrios winced. "I. . .I apologize, My Lord. I haven't been entirely truthful with you."

"With what?" Xander questioned him as he tried to take a step forward. His foot slipped on a wet plank and he would have fallen if Spiros and I hadn't caught him.

"Easy there, *Nester*. You are not as young and healthy as you believe yourself to be," Spiros scolded him.

Darda picked through the rubble and plucked the bell box from the planks which she then tucked under her arm. "We must lay him down," she insisted.

Kyrios jerked his head over his shoulder at the house. "He can have my bed in there, and I'll explain everything while my wife fetches some soup for you all and some dry clothes."

I glanced down at my companions and myself. We were all soaked from our watery ordeal, so soaked, in fact, that we dripped over the wet boards. I was relieved that my unique fae clothing kept the parts of my body it covered dry, but my hair and exposed skin was soaked and chilled to the bone.

MYTHS BEYOND DRAGONS

Kyrios led us into the house through its proper back door. The rooms were small, but cozy due to the several fireplaces that flickered with flames.

A pretty, petite young woman peeked out of the kitchen and her eyes widened out our bedraggled group. "By all the gods!" Two children, a girl and a boy, peeked around both sides of her dress and gaped at us.

"Some warm soup for these visitors, Mother, and all the blankets you can find," Kyrios requested. She nodded and ducked back into the kitchen, taking the young ones with her.

We hurried into the largest of the two bedrooms and laid Xander down on the homespun quilts. Chairs were gathered around the large fireplace. I dragged one close to the bed while my companions warmed themselves by the fire. Bowls of soup were soon in coming, brought by the pretty young woman. Her two young children marched behind her like ducklings and each carried a platter, one of breads and another of a half dozen cups of steaming tea.

I smiled at one of the kids, the little girl, as she offered me a cup. "Thank you," I whispered. She blushed and curtsied before she hurried to my companions.

Kyrios brought out spare blankets from a hope chest at the foot of the bed and passed them around. "I'll be glad to give you what clothes you need."

Xander sat up in the bed with a bowl of soup in his lap and shook his head. "We would rather be given answers."

Kyrios's wife paused in handing out the bowls and glanced at her husband. "Kyrios-?"

He held up his hand and shook his head. "We couldn't keep it a secret forever, Mother, and I for one will be glad to stop deceiving our lord."

Her eyes widened and she turned to Xander. "Our lord-?" Xander nodded.

The poor woman's legs failed her and she tumbled to the ground. Fortunately, all the bowls were passed around so only the platter fell with her, but her fainting spell sent our group into another flurry of panic.

"Mother!" Kyrios yelled as he rushed over to his wife.

"Mama!" her children cried out as they abandoned their platters and hurried to their parent.

Darda knelt beside the pale woman and smiled down into her tense face. "It is merely a fainting spell. I imagine her own drink will do her the better." She lifted Kyrios's wife into her arms and tipped the cup of tea against her lower lip. A bit of the drink slipped into her mouth and the woman choked. Her eyes fluttered open and she looked around at the familiar and unfamiliar faces in a half daze.

Kyrios slipped his arms beneath her and helped her to her feet. "Go to the kitchen, Mother."

His wife grasped his hands and shook her head. "But it's my fault as much as yours! I can't let you take all the blame!"

"What blame is there to be had?" Xander spoke up.

Kyrios sighed and looked in Xander's direction. "We have been using a portal for our own means, My Lord."

Xander's eyebrows crashed down. "Against the laws of the realms?"

His wife whipped her face toward Xander and shook her head. "It was my idea, My Lord! My husband was against it at the beginning!"

Xander held up his hand so that she was silenced before he turned his attention to Kyrios. "Where is this portal?"

Kyrios nodded at the floor. "In the cellar. It appeared there four months ago."

Tillit wrinkled his piggish nose. "In a cellar? I've never heard of one appearing below ground before."

"And it's not the only one," Kyrios continued as he looked over our entire group. "There have been a half dozen found near the dike along the lake over those same four months, and four of them were found only in the last four weeks."

"Four? So many?" Darda gasped.

He nodded. "Yes. Their appearance has coincided with every burst of wind along the lake, but beyond that we can't see any other reason for their appearing."

I glanced at Xander. His brow was furrowed and there was an intense expression on his face.

Kyrios's wife rushed up to Xander and fell to her knees beside the bed. She clutched one of his hands in both of hers and tears streamed down her cheeks as she looked into his eyes. "Please spare us, My Lord! For the sake of our children please don't report our wickedness to the priests! They would never allow us to return to them!"

Xander lay his free hand atop hers and smiled down at the weeping woman. "I will swear upon my honor not to tell another soul if you will show us this portal."

Her face brightened with a smile and she bowed her head to him. "Anything, My Lord! Anything!"

Kyrios walked up to her and set his hands on her quivering shoulders. "Mother, the children," he reminded her.

She raised her head and looked over at her children. They stood side-by-side in front of Darda and watched their mother's pleas with wide eyes and pale faces.

She stood and hurried over to them where she set her hands on their opposite shoulders. "Come, children. Let's pick up this mess and leave Daddy alone to entertain our guests."

The mother and children picked up their platters and left. Kyrios watched them go with soft eyes before he returned his attention to Xander as he lay on the bed beside him. "My Lord, I am truly-"

Xander raised a hand and shook his head. "There is no need for an apology. I, too, can understand the temptation to use portals, but they are dangerous because they may grow larger and swallow the surrounding area."

Kyrios shook his head. "But it hasn't grown larger, not an inch over this whole time. We've measured it carefully every day and would have stopped if it had grown larger."

"That does not mean it will not grow over a great amount of time," Darda argued.

"Or maybe smaller," Tillit spoke up.

Darda whipped her head to him and frowned. "Everyone knows portals do not shrink."

He folded his arms across his chest and shrugged. "Why not? They disappear."

She put her hands on her hips and scowled at him. "Have you seen one shrink?"

He grinned and shook his head. "No. Have you seen one grow?" Darda's expression darkened, but she turned away without a reply.

Xander returned his attention to Kyrios. "May we see this portal?"

Kyrios nodded. "Of course, My Lord. Any time you wish."

"Then now," Xander insisted as he set his bowl on the nightstand and swung his legs over the side of the bed.

"Wait a second!" I snapped as I rushed over to his bedside, spilling some tea in the process. I blocked his way with a dripping cup and my fury. "You nearly had your wings torn off and your ribs *are* bruised, so you lay down there while we go look."

Xander frowned up at me. "I am healed enough to-"

"To remain in bed for a few minutes longer," Spiros spoke up as he came to stand by my side in a united front that blocked Xander from standing. The captain smiled down at me. "Take Tillit and Darda with you. Tillit knows as much about portals as any priest."

"More," Tillit objected.

I grinned and pushed my hot tea cup into Xander's hands. "Hold these for me until I get back, and you-" I turned to Kyrios and gave him a friendly push toward the door, "-lead the way."

Xander spilled a little of my tea on him and sputtered out a few words. "B-but what of our partnership?"

I paused in the doorway with Tillit and Darda behind me, and Kyrios in front of me, and smiled back at him. "It's still there, but let's just say it's paused on account of injury. Besides, we'll be right back."

I hurried my group out the door as Xander tried to rise. Spiros stabbed a finger into his side as I lost my view of the room. A sharp yelp followed by the ouch of hot tea in a lap made my smile widen.

CHAPTER 23

Tillit sidled up beside me and studied my expression with a grin of his own. "You're getting quite devilish, Miriam."

Darda sighed and shook her head. "She is becoming more and more like Xander's mother."

I bowed my head to her. "I'll take that as a compliment."

The corners of her lips twitched up as she returned my bow. "As you should."

Kyrios guided us out to the back of the house and to the open cellar doors. A set of wooden stairs led into the darkness beneath the home. We descended into the unknown and found ourselves in a dirt root cellar. The room was the same shape as the square house. Oil lamps hung from the walls and illuminated a stack of crates to our left. To our right was a square wood box some three feet high and four feet square.

MYTHS BEYOND DRAGONS

Kyrios scooped up some wet soil brought in from the many boots that had trodden on the dirt floor, grabbed a lamp that hung near the crates, and walked over to the box. We followed him and stood around the box which turned out to be a potato pit some eight feet deep. I could make out the spuds around the sides of the box, but in the center was only darkness.

"My children came down here four months ago to fetch some roots and they found the pit nearly empty," Kyrios explained to us as he lowered the lamp into the hole. The light revealed a small portal some two feet in circumference. "Our roots were gone and this was here."

Tillit glanced over his shoulder at the stack of crates. "I'm guessing you know where your roots went."

Kyrios gave a nod. "Yes. My little boy was very curious and leaned too far over so that he fell in. His sister screamed and alerted Mother and me. We hurried down and found he'd disappeared, so I tied a rope around my waist and followed him." He dropped the clump of mud into the portal and the dirt disappeared. "We found ourselves at the bottom of the path close to Alexandria. I flew us back and informed Mother of what we found. We had a large shipment of fish that were spoiling from lack of men to handle the horses down the path, so she suggested we lower the crates through the portal and deliver them. That was the start of our trade."

Tillit leaned one elbow on the pit wall and arched an eyebrow at our host. "Why'd you fly back up here? Why not go back through the portal?"

Kyrios nodded at the vortex. "The other side of this won't take you anywhere but to the end of the path, like a loop."

"So the portal that sent us here will probably what? Send us back here?" I guessed.

"If that new portal you came through works like the others in the area then that's how it should work," he agreed.

Tillit snorted. "How can anyone be sure when they're sprouting like weeds?"

Kyrios picked up some more mud and tossed it once in his hand. "Let us see."

We walked back up the stairs and the short yards to our own swirling portal. The remains of the ship had been set aside by the stable men so that we stood right in front of it. It was five times the size of the portal in the root pit.

Tillit looked forlornly from the vortex to the remains of his ship and sadly shook his head. "It's a wonder she fit at all."

I glanced between ship and portal, and furrowed my brow. "It is a lot larger than the other portal, isn't it? I wonder why."

"They're all different sizes," Kyrios spoke up as he nodded to our portal. "But this is the biggest by far."

Tillit shook himself from his forlorn revelry and looked to our guide. "Well, throw the mud and we'll see how this one works."

Kyrios drew his arm back and threw the watery dirt into the portal. The mud was gone for only a fraction of a second before it sped out of the portal and flew into Tillit's face. He fell flat onto his rear and sputtered on a few bits of mud.

Darda chuckled as she watched Tillit sit up and wipe the mud from his face. "It appears we have solved that mystery."

Tillit cleared his eyes and glared at her. "You don't have to rub the mud deeper into my face. It's gone up my nostrils far enough." I helped him up and he wiped himself off before he turned his attention to Kyrios. "Your lovely wife's soup would most certainly hit the spot now, but I hope not as badly as the mud."

Kyrios smiled and nodded. "Not quite as badly."

We returned to the house with me in the lead. Our group wasn't especially quiet, but whatever noise we made was drowned out by the laughing of the two children as they helped their mother in the kitchen. I reached the partially shut door to the bedroom and stretched out my hand to open it when I heard my name mentioned.

"Miriam must not know," Xander insisted.

"She would never keep such a secret from you," Spiros argued.

"I do not wish to alarm her."

I steadied myself and swung the door open. The two guilty parties whipped around to face me and I grinned at them. "Alarm away!"

Xander pursed his lips and turned his face away from me. Spiros stood from his seat beside the bed and smiled at us. "What have you discovered?"

I strode up to the foot of the bed and crossed my arms over my chest as I glared at my dragon lord. "That there's a black hole in the root pit, our portal only leads to here, and that you two are hiding something from us."

Xander shook his head. "We are hiding nothing from the group."

"All right, then you're hiding something from *me*," I corrected myself.

Xander's eyes flickered past me and fell on Kyrios. Tillit noticed the look and turned to our host with a smile. "Would you be so kind as to ask your wife for more tea? Ours is a little cold and I see Our Lord's cup is nearly empty."

Kyrios smiled and bowed his head. "Of course." He slipped away and Tillit closed the door behind him.

I returned my attention to Xander. "Well? What is it?"

Xander pursed his lips, but sighed. "On the lake when I manifested my wings I. . .I felt a terrible instinct inside of me."

"And?" I persisted.

He frowned. "And I did not have complete control of that instinct."

"You controlled it just fine in the boat," I pointed out.

Xander narrowed his eyes. "I merely unfurled my wings-"

"And brought your claws out," I added.

"-and if I attempt to change into my full dragon form the instinct may be stronger than my control," he finished.

Spiros resumed his seat beside Xander and smiled at the dragon lord. "Do you recall when we were children practicing our first transformation?"

Xander arched an eyebrow. "What has that to do with the current circumstances?"

Spiros's grin widened. "There is quite a bit of instinct to overcome during the first transformation. If I recall correctly, you nearly ate your father."

Tillit and I snorted. Darda sighed and shook her head.

Xander frowned. "That was a less powerful instinct than this new one."

"But you are a more powerful dragon lord," he argued.

Xander didn't look convinced, so I stepped around to the side of the bed opposite Spiros and took a seat beside Xander. I set my hand atop his and smiled at him. "And you have a powerful mate at your side."

"And a smart sus," Tillit spoke up.

"I will not leave you," Darda added.

The corners of Xander's lips twitched up, but he shook his head. "I feel I am endangering all of you."

I squeezed his hand and grinned. "Well, if you get too dragony than we'll be here to slap some sense into you. Literally."

He winced. "That is what I fear." Our small group broke into laughter.

When our merriment had died down Tillit cleared his throat. "Now that we are all in good spirits I'm afraid I have to remind everyone that we have more than just a war and a god to contend with. There's now the portals."

"Kyrios mentioned there was six," I reminded everyone.

"Plus our own," Darda added.

Xander looked to Tillit. "Have you ever heard of such an occurrence?"

Tillit shook his head. "Nope, and I doubt anyone else has, either. If the priests found out about this they'd have heart attacks and then throw everyone within a hundred miles into the interrogation dungeons below Hadia."

"There may be a pattern to their locations that may lead us to the source," Spiros suggested.

I grinned. "And we could use the map to find them."

Spiros pulled out the Zoi map and gave it a little flick. A few specks of water slid off it like it was laminated, and he then spread it over Xander and the bed. He pressed his hand on the lake and expanded the view so we could see the whole of the southern bank. The rocks were clearly visible, and we could even a few small crabs scuttle across the heavy boulders.

I frowned. "Where's the portal?"

Spiros pointed at a spot half along the rock dike. "It should be at this point, but I cannot see any evidence of it being there."

"Maybe it disappeared after we used it?" I suggested.

Spiros shook his head. "That is not likely. While portals are fickle I do not believe one that size would have disappeared so quickly."

"But maybe this one's different," I insisted. "I mean, what do we really know about these portals, anyway? Just that they send somebody, or something, to some other place, right?"

Xander leaned back and rubbed his chin in his hand. "I have never known a portal to disappear, and to be cautious we should assume the portal is still there." I frowned, but said nothing as he pursed his lips. "Assuming that, however, then this should not be possible. The map is capable of showing all that is within my realm."

"What if it's not in your realm?" Tillit spoke up.

We all turned to him, and Darda frowned. "Of course it is in Lord Xander's realm. The dike is very well within his boundaries."

Tillit shook his head. "I'm not meaning physically in his realm, but between realms, or worlds, if you want. Maybe these portals aren't really a part of any world so the map doesn't consider them a part of Xander's realm."

Xander dropped his hand and nodded. "That is not an impossibility, but we might prove that with a view of another known portal."

He set his hand over the stables operated by Kyrios and a clear image of the small settlement came into view. The rear view of the house was very visible, but the portal through which we'd traveled from the lake to the outpost was not.

"I guess that means we really can't see them," I commented as Spiros lifted his hand and rolled up the map.

"Then we will have to search for them, but after we have dealt with the god," Xander suggested.

Darda patted the box that sat on the chair beside her. "He shall be dealt with, and I shall enjoy watching him vanish from our world."

"*If* he vanishes. Maybe he implodes," I suggested.

Tillit wrinkled his nose. "For once, I hope Darda's right."

She glared at him. "For once *you* are right."

MYTHS BEYOND DRAGONS

"Whoever is correct we must hurry back to the city," Xander insisted as he stood. His legs were a little shaky, but held him. The door opened and Kyrios stepped inside with a platter of steaming mugs in one hand. "Thank you, Kyrios, and could you saddle your fastest horses. We must return to the city as soon as we can."

Kyrios set the platter on a small table beside the door and bowed his head. "They will be ready in ten minutes."

CHAPTER 24

Kyrios slipped out and Darda passed around the warm mugs. I had hardly clutched my cup in both hands and tipped the mouth against my own when there came a cry of surprise from outside. A window stood on the wall behind the bed. I hurried around the bed as Spiros and Xander leapt at the window. They shoved their shoulders together as they fought for a view.

I stood on my tiptoes behind them and looked over their broad shoulders. The view showed only the side of the house and a little in both directions. We could just make out the end of the stables. A crowd of the stable hands was gathered at the far corner.

"Spiros!" Xander called as he rushed to the door.
"Yes, sir!" Spiros replied as he followed on his heels.
"Hey! Wait a sec!" I called to them as they sped out of the room.

MYTHS BEYOND DRAGONS

We all put our cups down and hurried after them to the far end of the stables. The hands turned at our coming and parted as Xander and Spiros pushed their way through to the front. I followed the pair and reached the front of the crowd.

A well with three-foot sides made of soft stones stood on the other side of the stables. Beside the well stood Kyrios, and he stared hard at a small mare that stood close to the well. She lifted her head with her mouth full of grasses and a pool of water that surrounded the low walls.

My mouth dropped open when I recognized that cud-chewer as Kyma, my wave-marked mare. "How'd she get here?" I spoke up.

Kyrios shook his head. "I have no idea. She's never come back without being returned by a client or one of my men. She's not *supposed* to come back without a rider."

I shrugged. "Well, I guess we need just four more horses."

Xander turned to Kyrios. "Have you readied them?"

Kyrios shook his head. "Not yet, but give my men and me a moment and we'll have them for you."

Soon we had four horses and my old mare at the ready, and set off for Pyschi. The trip was a little shorter due to our quicker pace, but the distance meant it was still late afternoon by the time we reached the threshold of the valley. Our little hill gave us a great view of the narrow land as the sun set, causing a light nearly as blinding as the sun to reflect off the rocking surface of the lake.

I turned away from the bright surface and looked to our left at the mountains. The herds of pani shifted and bleated. The herdsman stood from their grassy spots and hopped off their post seats. All their attentions looked up the mountain.

I followed their gazes and noticed a winding path that led down the mountain and stopped fifty feet from the last fence. A wide, orange serpent slithered down the trail and widened at the foot where I could see the body of the serpent. It was short and black, and I could see its body flickered between red and orange colors.

I pointed at the trail. "What's that?"

My companions followed my finger. Xander stood on his stirrups and frowned. "Those are torches."

"Carried by a short people, by the measure of their torches with the fence posts," Spiros added.

Darda gasped. "Are we to be invaded by the dwarves as well as gods and Black dragons?"

"We shall see why they have come," Xander replied as he kicked the sides of his horse.

His steed sprinted down the short slope and toward the fences with us close at its tail. The trees were too close on the side of venture through, so we had to hoof it across the fields. We reached the fence as the herdsman took up their horns from their sides and blew them. The sounds echoed off the mountain walls and rushed into the city. The guards at the front gate hurried to the corrals, but we beat them to the gate by five yards.

Xander leapt down from his horse and wrapped the reins around a fence pole before he climbed the fence itself. We followed behind him, but he was much faster than even Spiros as he raced across the pasture to the far gate. The pani moved against us in the opposite direction, bawling as they passed.

The torches on the plains now numbered in the dozens with countless others still up and down the trail. They cast their flickering light the trees, grass, and stone against the growing darkness. They created a circle with an empty but illuminated area in their center.

Xander reached the gate where a half dozen of the herdsman guarded the entrance with their staffs held tightly in their hands. Spiros reached Xander, and a few seconds later Darda and I joined them.

MYTHS BEYOND DRAGONS

The circle of dwarves parted and created an opening. One of their own, torch in hand, strode over to us. The dragons stiffened.

I leaned forward on the fence and squinted at the figure. "Isn't that the dwarf chief person?"

The person who walked toward us was indeed the same dwarf with whom we'd had dealings with on the Heavy Mountain. He stopped ten feet from us and bowed his head. "A pleasure to be seeing you again, Lord Xander." The herdsman around us whipped their heads to my dragon lord and gaped at him.

Xander pursed his lips as he swept his eyes over the hundreds of dwarves that crowded the trail and edge of the fields. At their hips tucked in their sashes were heavy axes. "I wish I could say the same, Amown, but I cannot think of any time I would be pleased to see several hundred of your strongest men, armed with axes, come to my territory.

Amown lifted his head and smiled. "You don't need to be worrying about us, Your Lordship. We've only come to talk to you."

Xander arched an eyebrow. "Who told you I was here?"

"I did," a voice spoke up.

A beautiful woman of thirty stepped out of the forest of torches and into the ring of fire. Her hair was as black as raven wings and her skin was as pale as death. She wore a long black overcoat that reached to the tops of her high black boots and was lined with black fur. Her under-attire was a black turtleneck sweater and black pants.

She stopped in the middle of the ring and gestured to us. "If you would come this way we can have a more-" her eyes flickered to the herdsman, "-*private* chat."

"Only a chat?" Xander challenged her.

She swept her hand over the dwarves. "You know as well as I the code of the dwarves. They would never harm a friend."

Xander opened the gate and stepped through. Spiros, Darda, and I quickly followed. Tillit, huffing and puffing, finally reached us. He groaned as we pulled away from him. "A little time," he wheezed. "That's all I ask."

Darda stopped, rolled her eyes and walked back to him. She grabbed his hand and dragged him along with her. We all entered the ring and the dwarves closed the entrance behind us.

The woman strode up to Xander and bowed her head. "Allow me to introduce myself. I am Salome, Lady of the Black." She lifted her head and as she did so she admired his body. "I was told the lord of Alexandria was handsome, but I didn't expect such a dragon as I see before me."

Xander pursed his lips. "How did you learn I was here?"

She winked at him. "I have my sources, ones my cousin would *kill* to get a hold of."

Xander glanced around at our torch-bearing surroundings. "You are violating the laws of the realms as laid out by our forefathers by bringing with you these armed dwarves."

The smile didn't slip from her lips as she folded her arms across her ample chest and shrugged. "What is an old law when a matter of the lordship of a realm is at stake?"

"Whatever plans you have to take the lordship, my people want no part of it," Xander snapped.

Salome laughed. "You cannot help but be involved! Our borders are connected, and so must be our fates. However-" she set her dainty fingers on his shoulder and walked around him in a circle like a cat with a mouse, "-you could finish all of this rather quickly."

He arched an eyebrow. "How?"

"Why, by siding with me and helping me do away with my troublesome cousin," she cooed.

Xander shrugged off her hand and stepped back so he stood at the head of our group. "I will not take sides in this quarrel, nor will I allow either of you to harm any of my subjects."

Salome crossed her arms over her chest and frowned at him. "You have all the looks of a god, but the intelligence of a worm." I ground my teeth together and took a step toward her, but Darda set her hands on my shoulders and held me back. "Do you honestly believe you can both keep out of the war *and* protect your people? The idea is laughable."

"I will do whatever it takes to protect my people, even if it means warring against you both," Xander swore.

Salome stepped back and tilted her head to one side as she studied him. "I had heard you'd gained some great powers in your fight against the Bestia Draconis, but I hardly think it would aid you in defeating *two* armies."

"He's not alone," I spoke up.

Salome's eyes fell on me and narrowed. "Ah, yes, his little fae Maiden. I have no doubt your powers are formidable against my cousin's fleet, but on land they-" she gestured to the dwarves, "-are the rulers of the battlefield."

"You want to test that out?" I challenged her.

She sighed and turned away from us. "This conversation is pointless. I can see there's no reasoning with you." She waved her hand. The wall of dwarves behind us opened to the pasture land. "Let us hope we shall not meet again, Lord Xander, until after I am made Lady of the Black land."

Xander pursed his lips, but bowed his head and turned away. I glared one last time at that haughty back of hers and followed him with my friends. We left the circle and the dwarves pressed together in a tight column of four wide. They marched back up the trail, joining their many brethren.

Xander watched them go with worry in his eyes. "I cannot see how this will end well."

Tillit glanced behind us toward the pasture and his face fell. "It's about to get worse."

CHAPTER 25

We followed his gaze and I felt my heart drop into my stomach. Across the fields, but quickly coming toward us, was three dozen Psychi guards on horseback. We stayed put with the herdsman close beside us so that the horsemen reached us in a few seconds and stopped some ten feet from where we stood.

The leader, a man with a thick staff and an extra-large sickle atop it, pointed his weapon at us. "Who are you and why did the dwarves retreat?"

Spiros made to step forward, but Xander raised his hand and moved to our front. "I am Xander, Lord of Alexandria."

A murmur went up among the horsemen as their leader arched an eyebrow. "Even if you are who you say you are, I have to ask for proof."

Xander nodded. "Of course."

MYTHS BEYOND DRAGONS

His wings sprouted from his back and stretched twenty feet on either side of him. The horses whinnied and reared back at such an impressive display.

The leader of the guards widened his eyes as he drew his horse back under his control. "By all the gods. . ."

"Will that suffice?" Xander asked him.

The leader nodded. "Y-yes, of course, My Lord, but why are you here and why did those dwarves come here?"

"They are apparently allies of Salome, lady of the Black dragons-" Xander informed him, "-and it is because of that conflict that I am here."

The man pursed his lips. "I'm glad you're here, then, My Lord. Captain Kokinos informed us of the trouble that was had at Omonoia earlier, so I've had my men prepare the ships for battle, especially after the message that was found a few days ago."

Xander arched an eyebrow. "What message?"

It was a message in a bottle, My Lord, that was found floating near the ships. It warned us that Psychi would be attacked and we should fear the Black dragons," he revealed.

"Was that the exact wording of the letter?" Spiros spoke up.

The leader pursed his lips. "Not exactly. I believe it the latter part was something closer to 'Beware the other,' but obviously we have no one to fear but the Black dragons."

Xander nodded. "Thank you, captain. My friends and I will remain in the city until this conflict is resolved. You may find us at the Tillit home, if that is familiar to you."

The captain nodded. "It is, My Lord. If I might ask your advice, My Lord, but do you want my men to remain in these fields in case the dwarves should attack?"

"I do not believe they will attack, but to ease the concerns of the citizenry an armed guard would be wise," Xander advised him.

The captain bowed his head. "Thank you, My Lord. If you will excuse us."

The captain led his men in dismounting and the group began to coordinate their watch. Xander glanced over his shoulder at us and nodded his head toward our horses. We followed him across the wide fields to our steeds.

Kyma impatiently pawed the ground as I neared her. I wrapped my arms around her neck and scratched behind her ear. "Sorry, old girl. We had some diplomacy to do." She snorted, but stopped pawing so I could mount her.

My companions did the same and Tillit drew his horse up to Xander's side. "I don't know about you, My Lord, but it's been a long day and this sus is nearly finished."

Xander looked up at the dark night sky and pursed his lips. "Unfortunately, you are right. Our day is used. Let us go partake of some food."

We meandered our way through the city to the district that harbored Tillit's ancestral home. Our group dismounted at his stables and the sus led us to the sliding door.

A foot before Tillit reached the entrance the door was flung open and a disheveled Mrs. Pachis stood in the doorway. Strands of her hair popped out of her tight bun and there was filth all over the front of her dress and apron. Her eyes were wide and her breathing rapid.

She threw herself over Tillit and wrapped her arms around his neck as she sobbed into his shoulder. "Mr. Tillit, I'm so sorry!"

He winced and pried her off so he held her at arm's length. "Sorry for what?"

Tears sprang into her eyes as Mrs. Pachis sniffled. "I don't know how it happened, but one of the horses got loose and wandered off. I've been looking for her all day and-" her gaze flickered past the sus and at my steed. Her eyes widened and her mouth dropped open. She whipped her head to Tillit, but pointed at my mare. "You've found her, Mr. Tillit! Where was the beast?"

Tillit chuckled. "It's more like she found us. She met us at the outpost."

Mrs. Pachis blinked at him. "The outpost, sir? All that way?" He nodded. She leaned back and shook her head. "I can't fathom it, sir. The door wasn't even open, and yet she was gone! I thought for sure we'd been burgled, but I couldn't understand why someone would take the worst of the horses."

Tillit smiled and patted her on the shoulder. "It's all fixed now, Mrs. Pachis, but for a fixing of dinner."

She nodded. "Of course. I'll have a feast ready for you in half an hour." She slipped back inside the stables and hurried through the side door into the house.

Tillit half-turned to our group and looked at my mare. "It looks like your mare has a knack for trouble like you."

I shrugged. "Maybe it rubbed off on me."

Tillit jerked his head to the interior of the stables. "Well, let's get inside." Our train of horses moved forward.

"Mister! Mister Spiros!" Spiros, who was ahead of me with Darda at my back, paused halfway through the door and looked to our left. Agatha, the little charge of Helle, hurried up to him. She put her fists on her hips and stomped her foot on the ground. "Where have you been, Mister Spiros?"

He knelt down so as to be face-to-face with her and smiled. "I have been saving the city."

Her stern expression softened a little. "From what?"

A devilish smile slipped onto his lips as he tucked his reins into his pants. "From a tickle monster." He whipped his hands out and tickled her armpits.

She screamed and giggled before she was able to step out of his reach. Her ill-temper was gone, vanquished by his playfulness. "You know, Helle was really worried about you. She won't say so, but she was. She even came here four times today to see if you were here."

"Well, how about you tell Helle I'll see both of you tomorrow?" he suggested.

Agatha smiled and nodded. "I will!" She turned to go, but paused and glanced over her shoulder at him. "She'll be home at nine, and don't you be late!"

"I will be there," Spiros promised.

Agatha waved to him and hurried off. Spiros straightened and looked around to find all of us staring at him with evil smiles. He arched an eyebrow. "We have an obligation to comfort the citizenry in this trying time."

I snorted. "I don't think 'comfort' is the right word."

"Everyone get inside before all the warm air in the stables gets out!" Tillit ordered us.

CHAPTER 26

We strode into the warm stables and cared for our steeds before our group walked into the house. I wasn't aware of how tired I was until I sat down in the dining room and stretched my legs. My muscles groaned and my weary bones cracked.

"Are you guys sure you can't invent airplanes and cars?" I asked my companions as they eased themselves into their own seats.

"If they would ease the road up the mountains I will be glad to violate some ancient, cross-world laws to produce them," Tillit spoke up as he shifted in his seat and winced.

Spiros glanced across the table at Xander who sat beside me. "Speaking of problems, we still have the god dilemma on top of the impending war."

I flinched. "I don't think I'm too eager to stick my hand back in the lake if we're just going to end up being shoved into a portal."

Darda nodded. "Yes. The next one might lead over a cliff."

Tillit sighed. "Well, then does anybody happen to know where we can find this god before he finds us?" He threw up his arms. "Heck, what do we even know about gods?"

Xander furrowed his brow. "Crates mentioned that the gods were like the fae in that their powers were derived from natural elements."

I tapped my chin and furrowed my brow. "If I were a wind god where would I be hiding?"

"The Windy Caves," Darda spoke up.

Spiros snapped his fingers. "That's it! Darda, you are a genius!"

She smiled and shrugged. "Only when the occasion arises."

"Which means we can safely assume that won't happen again for another dragon's life," Tillit teased her.

She glared at him. "At least mine comes *once* in a life."

"Not to interrupt this nice squabble, but could anybody tell me a little more about these caves?" I spoke up.

Xander shook his head. "There is little to tell. The winds have always been fiercest along the northern shores of the lakes where the caves reside so that no one has ever gone into them."

"So no map?" I guessed.

"Can you see what lies behind the rocks?" Xander asked Spiros.

Spiros shook his head. "The map only works for that which is along the ground. If we go down into these tunnels we will be traveling without a guide."

"Then we will be as doomed in those caves as on the lake," Darda commented.

It was Tillit's turn to glare at her. "Your optimism is astounding."

MYTHS BEYOND DRAGONS

She narrowed her eyes at him. "Can you see any other options?"

Xander stood and looked at each of us in our turn. "We have had a long day. Perhaps a night of rest will help us think of an alternate plan."

Tillit stood and stretched his legs. "The kitchen's open to anyone who wants it. I know I'll be digging into Mrs. Pachis's world-famous blood pudding."

I stuck out my tongue. "I think I just lost my appetite."

Darda stood and set her hands on my shoulders as she smiled down at me. "I will fetch you some proper food and bring it to your room." She glanced up at Xander. "Should I make that meal for two?"

He nodded. "Yes. I am a little hungry."

We broke apart into our groups, Xander and I upstairs and the others to the kitchen to harass the chef. I stumbled over half the steps and shuffled through the door Xander graciously opened for me. I plopped myself on the end of the bed and fell backwards onto the sheets.

"Who knew going for a boat ride would give us that much trouble?" I mused.

Xander took a seat beside me and smiled down at me. "You did have to conjure several of your dragons, and one of them had to carry Tillit."

I snorted. "That's true." I turned my face toward him and looked him over. "So how are your ribs?"

He looked down at his chest and pressed his hand against his ribs. "They are completely healed. I must admit there are some benefits to the Sæ. Without its waters I would not have healed so quickly."

I arched an eyebrow. "You know, there's something that's been bugging me since we left that stone fortress."

"What is it?" he asked me.

I looked up into his curious face. "It's about how Spiros proved who he was. What was with that scar on his chest?"

Xander looked ahead and pursed his lips. "I believe you know some of the particular of the war between the dragon lords some fifty years ago."

"Only enough to fill a cookie jar," I quipped.

"I was made lord on the death of my parents. At the time Spiros was one of my bodyguards, but upon my ascension he was inducted into the royal guards and placed among those of the first line."

"And that means what?" I asked him.

"The first line are those who go into battle with the lord, and it is he who leads the charge. Because of that Spiros was among those with me on that fateful day when the five armies faced the Red Dragon at the High Castle. Our foe was a formidable dragon, a giant even among dragon lords, and no less formidable was his second-in-command. That soldier was not only a brute but also a master of strategy. He lured my personal guards and me into a trap around the far side of the castle where the trees were thickest. We had been chasing a large group in the trees when they parted and revealed a clear-cut area with a line of Red dragons waiting for us, the second among them. We fought as hard as we could, but we were outnumbered." He paused and closed his eyes. "Many old friends died that day."

I sat up and cupped his chin in my hand. "I'm sorry. I didn't mean to remind you."

He set his hand over mine and opened his eyes to smile down at me. "Do not regret asking me. I am grateful to have someone with whom I can speak about these matters. As I said, many fell on both sides until only a few of us remained. The second made to attack me with his heavy sword. Mine was long broken. I had no way to defend myself. Then Spiros arrived. He flew in from the trees where he had broken through the guarding lines and flew in front of me. The strike meant to kill me was instead his to bear. He dropped to the ground, but not before he tossed his sword to me." He clenched his teeth and his eyes hardened. "I cut that dragon asunder and he fell in two pieces beside my friend. I though Spiros was dead-who could survive such a wound as he had?-and after the loss of my parents he was my closest companion. I-" he closed his eyes and shook his head, "-I had nothing more to lose. Filled with rage and grief, I killed my foes and broke from the trap. The Red Dragon flew over the High Castle in eagerness to find a worthy opponent. I flew to him, cutting down any who blocked my path, and came to him. We dueled-even to this day I cannot say for how long-and in the end I was the victor, but it seemed to me to be an empty victory."

"So how'd Spiros make it?" I wondered.

A small smile slipped onto his lips. "Prior to our leaving Alexandria his father has pleaded with Spiros to wear a special rope armor he had braided for him. Spiros was reluctant, but eventually agreed. It was that armor that saved him. The intricate knots had slowed the strength of the sword cut, blunting its killing intent. Still, he was gravely wounded and it was only through Apuleius's healing skill, and much stitching, that he survived."

"He really took one for you, didn't he?"

He nodded. "Yes. Greater than you can guess, for you see dragons, even in our human forms, naturally have very tough skin, but for Spiros the flesh over his wound is very weak. A single lucky strike by a sword or even a mere tap may reopen the wound and cause him to bleed to death."

My eyes widened. "You mean he's been running around with us all this time while a little tap of a sword could kill him?"

"Yes."

The color drained from my face. "How can he do it? I mean, how can he keep going into these dangerous places knowing he's that vulnerable?"

Xander tilted his head to one side and studied my face with a teasing smile. "Do you not do the same in your frail human body?"

I frowned and slapped his chest. "I'm doing it for you, remember?"

"As is he, and for all those for whom he cares," Xander pointed out.

I leaned my side against his and pursed my lips. "I guess you can't judge a book by its cover, huh?"

Xander arched an eyebrow, but smiled down at me. "I have not heard that saying before, but I find it very appropriate."

I closed my eyes and sighed. "Of course. Everyone knows I'm the perfect wit."

He chuckled. "And the perfect modest Maiden."

CHAPTER 27

We supped on the food Darda brought us and then went to bed. I was asleep almost before my head touched the pillow, but my rest was not to be a peaceful one. My mind was willing, but my ears decided they weren't done for the day.

A soft whisper of noise drifted over my ears. I wrinkled my nose and buried myself deeper into the covers. The warmth of Xander's body was very inviting, but my brain was slowly waking to low sounds.

I groaned and creaked open one eye. The small bedroom was dark, but a small fire still burned in the fireplace on my side of the bed. I could see nothing stir, but the sound grew louder. It was a noise like many whispers, and one of them stood out from the rest.

"*Phrixus. Phrixus.*"

I growled and flung aside the covers to sit up. "All right, who's there?"

Xander stirred beside me and glanced over his shoulder. "What is it?"

"*Phrixus. Phrixus, where are you?*"

I shook my head. "I don't know, but it sure wants me to find out."

I stood and walked over to the fireplace where I turned to face the room. Nothing moved save the shadows that danced in tune with the fire.

"*Phrixus, please don't do this.*"

"Who's Phrixus?" I called out. There was a tremble in the air and then I felt a sense of nothingness as though the voice had vanished. I ran a hand through my hair and shook my head. "I'm going mad. Now I'm evening imagining myself talking to voices of people who aren't there."

"Phrixus ?" Xander repeated as he climbed out of bed.

I nodded. "Yes, Phrixus. I kept hearing somebody call that name, but I think they just left."

He reached my side and studied the room. "I saw nor heard nothing."

I arched my eyebrow as I glanced up at him. "Nothing?"

He shook his head. "No, but you have heard voices when I heard nothing, as when we were at Alexandria by the lake."

I snapped my fingers. "Remember what Crates said? About needing to listen to the voices of the gods? Maybe Phrixus *is* a god! Maybe he's *the* god we're looking for."

He furrowed his brow. "Phrixus. . .Phrixus. . .the name is vaguely familiar to me in the days when I was young. I believe it was my mother who spoke it."

"So maybe Darda would know what it means?" I guessed.

He smiled and wrapped his arm around my back. "Let us have her join us in this wonderful midnight party."

I grinned and bowed my head, and together we strode out of our room and to the door of Darda's domain. Xander rapped on the hard wood.

"What is it?" came the groggy voice of my maidservant.

"I wish to ask you a question of my childhood," Xander called out.

There came an uncharacteristic groan followed by Darda running into some heavy furniture. The door creaked open and she peeked her head out. Her hair was mussed and her eyes were bleary as she stared from Xander to me and back to him. "Really, Xander, I thought you had gotten past being frightened by nightmares many years ago."

Xander chuckled. "This is not my nightmare, but that of Your Lady."

Darda's eyes widened and she whipped her head to me. "What is the matter?"

I grasped her hands and shook my head. "It's nothing that serious. Xander just wanted to know if the name Phrixus sounded familiar to you."

She wrinkled her nose. "Phrixus? I do recall a tale Lady Cate would tell to the young visitors of the city of a young man who rode a ram over the waters."

I looked up at Xander and grinned. "You remember what that god was wearing?"

He nodded. "Yes. A cloak made from a ram."

"And he was riding it over the waters," I added. I folded my arms over my chest and furrowed my brow. "So now we've probably got our culprit, but I don't see how that helps us."

"Perhaps tomorrow we will think of a way, but for the moment let us rest," Xander insisted as he set his hand on the lower part of my back and guided me back to our room.

We slipped back into bed, but a troublesome thought tickled my brain. Xander's back faced me, so I poked it. "Xander?"

"Mmm?" he replied.

"If that Phrixus really is the god who tried to kill us, then who do you think was calling his name?" I asked him.

Xander yawned. "Perhaps another god that still remains on our plane."

I lay on my back and stared up at the ceiling. The soft sound of Xander's breathing soothed my tired mind. Sleep drifted over me, but not before one last thought teased me: if that was another god, why was it so much louder than I'd heard before?

A new day shone down on the city and beckoned all to come bask in its warm glory. I ignored it and tucked myself deeper into the sheets. Unfortunately, I couldn't ignore the strong hand that shook my shoulder.

"Miriam," Xander whispered.

"Just ten more hours. . ." I murmured.

He chuckled and rocked me harder. "In another ten hours it will be the time to sleep."

I peeked open one of my eyes and set my gaze on him. "You promise?"

"When dealing with gods I can make no promise," he replied.

I sighed and sat up, groggy in the head and aching in the body. I ran a hand through my disheveled hair and groaned. "I feel like I was sucked into a wormhole and spat back out again."

Xander strode to the door, but paused and half-turned to me. "In essence, yes, but I will await you downstairs."

MYTHS BEYOND DRAGONS

    He exited the room. I flung aside the covers and looked down at myself. My clothes consisted of a long, thick nightgown. I focused my attention on the cloth and my clothes shifted to the appropriate dress, unwrinkled and form-fitting. I smiled and gave a nod before I hopped out of bed, ready to take on the world, or at least one god.
    How wrong I was.

CHAPTER 28

Unfortunately, that was in the future and at the present I hurried downstairs to meet my friends. They were seated at the dining table with a sumptuous feast laid before them.

Mrs. Pachis was just finishing up the serving. Her brow was furrowed and she shook her head as she spoke under her breath. "It beats me how that beast escaped. . ."

I sat down beside Xander and glanced at the window. "What time is it?"

"A little past nine," Tillit surmised.

A sly smile slipped onto my lips as my eyes flickered to Spiros. "I don't think Helle's going to like that."

A hard rap on the door caught our attention. Mrs. Pachis passed the dining room doorway and we heard the creak of the front door and her voice in the hall. "Why, hello there. Won't you two come in?"

MYTHS BEYOND DRAGONS

I noticed Spiros swallow fast before he leapt to his feet. Agatha appeared in the doorway with a frown on her lips, and attached to her was the more reluctant Helle. The little girl dragged her companion into the room, around the table, and stopped in front of Spiros.

"You promised!" she scolded him.

The corners of his lips twitched upward as he bowed his head. "Forgive me. My friends were in great need of rest after our perilous adventure yesterday."

Agatha's eyes widened. "Perilous adventure?" She furrowed her brow and looked up at Helle. "What's 'perilous' mean?"

Helle's face was pale and her gaze remained on Spiros as she answered. "It means dangerous, but I hope you're only jesting."

Spiros shook his head. "I fear not, my lady, and there is something we wish to ask of you."

Tillit glanced at his housekeeper who nodded and walked forward to the table and looked to the young girl. "Would you like some cookies, Miss Agatha?"

Agatha whipped her head around and her eyes brightened. "Yes, please!" She looked up at Helle. "May I?"

Helle nodded. "Yes, but not too many."

"Yippee!" Agatha raced from the room with Mrs. Pachis far behind.

Spiros slipped the chair beside him out and Helle reluctantly sat down. Spiros turned his seat so he half-faced her and looked her in the eyes. "Miss Helle-"

"Just Helle. I would like it if you called me that," she pleaded.

He smiled and nodded. "Helle, I feel I must tell you that we are not mere adventurers. We have come on a most important mission to save Psychi from a terrible power."

She stiffened and clenched her hands in her lap. "What sort of power?"

"A god threatens the lakes," Xander spoke up.

Helle raised her head at him and pursed her lips. "*A god?*"

He nodded. "Yes. We must stop him before he wreaks havoc on the inhabitants of both cities, but in order for us to do that we must find him."

She shook her head. "I-I'm sure I can't help."

Spiros set his hand atop hers and smiled at her. "I know we are asking you much of you, but you are the only one to whom we can turn. Agatha told us you were familiar with the shores, and so we turn to you begging for your help."

Helle returned her attention to him and bit her lower lip. "What do you wish to know?"

"We suspect this god hides in the Windy Caves, but there are no maps or personal knowledge of that shore to show us a way into them," Spiros explained.

Helle nodded. "I will help you, but you must promise me one thing."

Spiros smiled. "Anything."

"The god must not come to harm."

We all started back, Spiros most of all. Tillit snorted. "You've got a pretty big heart to be pitying someone who's trying to destroy your city."

Helle swept her eyes over all of us. "I know it's a strange request, but I know in my heart that violence is not the way." Helle wrapped her hands around one of Spiros's and looked into his eyes. "Please. I beg you to be kind to him."

Spiros pursed his lips, but nodded. "I swear on my honor he will not be harmed."

Xander's eyebrows crashed down. "Captain Spiros, do you forget your duty to the city and its inhabitants?"

"But I'm an inhabitant," Helle insisted as she met his stern gaze. "I only ask for pity. Please grant me this one wish and I will do whatever you ask of me."

Xander frowned, but nodded. "Very well. Spiros, the Zoi map." Spiros drew the map from his vest and stretched it over the table.

Helle's eyes widened as he zoomed in on the whole of the northern shoreline of the lake. "What beautiful magic."

"Touch the spot where the entrance is to be found," Spiros instructed her.

Helle hardly studied the map for a second before she tapped on one particular point halfway along the shore. The map zoomed in and revealed a flat rock with a heavy shadow beneath its load. "There. That is an entrance into the Caves."

"Will it lead us as deep as the caves run?" Xander asked her.

She nodded. "Yes, and it connects to many of the other tunnels."

Tillit leaned forward and squinted at the area. "How many other entrances are there?"

Helle shook her head. "None that lead to more than dead ends."

His eyes flickered to her. "How'd you learn so much about these caves with all that wind blowing through them? Men have tried and had their skulls bashed in."

Helle swallowed hard. "I-well, that is, the winds have been very calm these past few months, so I explored them a great deal."

"Did you ever see this god in the caves?" Tillit asked her.

She shook her head. "I only saw my reflection." We looked at her with blank expressions. She cringed. "That is, there are a great deal of puddles in the caves. I saw my reflection in those many pools."

"Thank you for your information," Xander spoke up. He stood from his chair and looked around at all of us. "We should go now. There might be a long day before us."

Helle rose and looked him in the eyes as she steadied herself. "Sir, if you wouldn't mind, but I'd like to come with you."

Spiros's face fell as he, too, stood. "You do not trust me to keep my word?"

She shook her head. "No. I. . . I have my reasons, among them that the caves are very deep and winding. You might become lost." She smiled up at him. "That alone is enough reason for me to go with you."

Tillit groaned as he stood, leaving before him an empty plate filled with crumbs. "Well, I've had a good last meal, so I suppose I'm ready."

Darda rose and turned her nose up at him. "You have had enough last meals to be for all of us."

He chuckled and patted his ample stomach. "A sus always has a hearty appetite. I think I have enough room for some of Mrs. Pachis's famous cookies, too."

Helle's eyes widened as she looked from Tillit back to Spiros. "Agatha! I'd completely forgotten about her! She can't be left alone-"

"Mrs. Pachis can take care of her until we get back," Tillit assured the young woman.

Helle smiled at him and bowed her head. "Thank you. You don't know what this means to me."

Tillit hitched up his pants. "It means it's time to leave. We'd better sneak out or Mrs. Pachis and Agatha will try to stop us."

We slipped out the front door as quiet as church mice and headed down the road. The city was hardly the stuff of Armageddon legend. People bustled up and down the streets to their shopping and work. Carts rolled by driven by lazy horses who plodded along the smooth stone streets. The air was as calm as sleeping children, and everyone was all smiles as they enjoyed the warm sun that hung in the cloudless sky.

MYTHS BEYOND DRAGONS

I sidled up to Xander and lowered my voice to a whisper. "Do you really think that god's out to get everybody?"

He shook his head. "I cannot say, but if the librarian is sure they are a threat to our world than they must leave."

I looked him over and pursed my lips. "I know Crates is supposed to be an expert on everything, but he might be wrong this one time."

Xander's eyes flickered down to me. "Do you recall how the god sought to kill us on the rocks?"

I winced. "On second thought, maybe he is a crazy lunatic." I glanced over my shoulder. Darda and Tillit grudgingly walked behind us because Spiros was preoccupied with his lady friend at the rear. My gaze fell on our young friend and I furrowed my brow. "She seems to think this god's a good guy, doesn't she?"

Xander stared ahead as he pursed his lips and gave a nod. "Yes."

I glanced up at him and arched an eyebrow. "And you don't like that."

He shook his head. "No."

"So why don't you like that? Maybe she's just being kind," I suggested.

"Have you ever known a woman to plead for the life of a stranger?" he asked me.

I face fell. "I see what you mean, but do you think she's hiding something bad from us?"

"We shall see."

CHAPTER 29

With Tillit's ship out of commission for an eternity we rented another ship, one of the newer models, from a grizzly local. He was gray-haired, what hair he had left, and sported an untamed gray beard.

"Where are ya taking her?" he asked us as he received his commission in gold coins handed to him by Tillit.

"To the Windy Caves," Xander revealed.

The man's eyes widened, stretching his weathered skin to a more youthful appearance. "Them? Then I'll be taking double my usual pay."

Tillit glared at him. "They're just as safe as any part of the lake on the off days, and today's an off day."

The captain shook his head. "It's not that I'm worried about, it's them caves,. A few folks have got curious since the winds died and took their ships over their to fish, but they only do it once before they've learned their lesson."

The sus snorted. "Did a few fish scare them off?"

MYTHS BEYOND DRAGONS

The sea swab glared at him. "No fish ever made a noise like what's been heard."

"What noise has been heard?" Xander asked him.

The grizzled man furrowed his withered brow and shook his head. "The tales that have been told to me about it say it's the cry of a madman and the wail of a banshee, all together in some horrible voice."

"Helle!"

We all turned around to see Helle fallen to her knees on the ground. Spiros held her in his arms and looked down at her in horror. Her face was as pale as a ghost and she clutched onto him like a drowning sailor.

"What is wrong, Helle?" he asked her.

She shook herself and gave him a weak smile. "I-I'm fine. It's just-I'm-the water-" she nodded at the large expanse of water that sparkled before us. "I'm terrified of it."

Spiros grasped one of her hands with his while his other one cradled her back. "I will be here by your side," he swore as he helped her stand.

She squeezed his hand and nodded. "I know, and thank you."

Xander returned his attention to the old sailor. "Have the sounds been heard recently?"

The man shook his head. "I don't know. Nobody goes near that place now. Now about my fee-"

Another handful of coins and we had our ship. Tillit took the helm while the rest of us took seats along the length of the ship. With one extra passenger we were forced to get a longer ship than our last so that there was another seat on which Darda could sit with the small bag that contained the Theos Chime. Spiros and Helle took another while Xander and I had the bow seat.

We sailed across the smooth waters with the sun shining brightly down on us. The lake sparkled like emeralds and a few fish leapt out of the water around us. A soft breeze was just strong enough to fill our sails and our spirits with its cool touch. I would've enjoyed it more if we hadn't been heading for the ominous foothills of the Heavy Mountains

I glanced over my shoulder at our crew and my gaze fell on Helle. Her eyes stared unblinkingly at the Windy Caves as they fast approached. I could see her body quivered like the last leaf on a dying tree. One of her hands gripped the side of the boat while the other lay clenched in her lap.

Spiros leaned toward her and wrapped her tight fist in his hand. She started back and whipped her head up to him. He smiled back at her, and she in turn managed a shaky smile. She loosened her death grip on the poor boat and swallowed a lump in her throat so that the rest of her body relaxed.

I snorted. Xander glanced at him and frowned. "What is humorous?"

I shrugged. "Oh, just remembering my first puppy love."

He arched an eyebrow. "'Puppy love?'"

I nodded. "Yeah, it means your first love."

"Was I that person?" he wondered.

I shook my head. "Not by a long shot." I furrowed my brow and tapped my chin. "I think I was about eight when it happened."

He started back. "Eight? Do humans fall in love so young?"

I laughed and shook my head. "Not really. I just thought he was cute, so I followed him along the playground for a few days until he told the teacher I was bothering him. That ended that relationship fast."

Xander studied me for a moment longer before he looked away and shook his head. "I will never understand humans."

I patted him on the shoulder. "Neither will I."

"We're almost there," Tillit spoke up.

We returned our attention to the steep slope of the Heavy Mountains. No trees grew up that vicious incline, and only a few pathetic bushes lined the shore. Large boulders and smaller rocks, castaways of the mountains, littered the waters within fifty feet of land. On land the mountain was speckled with cave entrances of various sizes and shapes. Some, like ours, were hidden beneath unsteady boulders. Others were out in the open, but half-cluttered with rubble.

The entrance we needed stood twenty feet up the rocky face. Between the cave and the edge of land was a minefield of stones and boulders, each designed to wound knees and stub toes.

Tillit parked our boat near one of the larger rocks that stuck out of the water some thirty feet from shore. "This is as close as I dare get. We'll have to fly the rest of the way."

Helle shrank back from the suggestion. "But I can't fly."

Darda furrowed her brow. "But you are a dragon, are you not? Your scent tells as much."

Helle nodded. "Yes, but-well, my wings don't work. They were-um-they were damaged in a rough wind storm, so I can't use them."

"I will carry you," Spiros offered.

Tillit grinned at Darda. "That means you get the pleasure of carrying me, dear Darda."

She glanced over her shoulder and wrinkled her nose at him. "'Pleasure' is *not* the right word."

I stepped onto the rock and turned to the boat and my companions. "How about I just do this?"

Six of my water dragons burst out of the water and surrounded the boat. Their necks were thick enough to carry even the heaviest of sus.

Helle gaped at them. "Water spirits." Her wide eyes fell on me. "You are a Mare fae?"

"Half of me is," I told her.

"Let us be off," Xander insisted as he straddled one of my dragons.

The others and I joined him, and my not-so-little pets swam us through the rocky waters and up the steep incline to the opening. Beneath the shadow of the rock was a rectangular entrance some ten feet wide and five feet tall. Xander reached the location first, and made to step off his steed and onto a small lip that stretched out from the entrance.

"Wait!" Helle shouted. Xander paused and turned to us as we joined him. Helle dismounted and bowed to him. "There are many dangers inside, so please allow me to lead you."

"You mean besides an angry god?" I asked her.

She nodded. "Yes. There are many floor shafts that lead below the water, and there are loose rocks that could tumble at any moment."

Xander gestured to the entrance. "Then by all means, lead the way."

We followed our guide into the mouth of the unknown. Tillit had thought ahead and brought a few torches which we lit so his and my weak eyes could see the interior.

It turned out we also had some help from some natural formations. The sunlight shot into the cave system and illuminated bright blue stones that were embedded in the floor, ceiling, and walls. They glowed, and their glowing reflected off the stones deeper in the cave so that a soft blue light gave us enough illumination to see the interior with our own eyes.

We stood in a small cavern some ten feet tall and twenty feet wide. A few holes pocketed the floor and led into long drops to floors below where we stood. In the walls were some half dozen tunnels of various mouth sizes. Some curved into the distance, others took sharp turns so that we couldn't see more than thirty feet down their path.

MYTHS BEYOND DRAGONS

A soft breeze came from the depths of those tunnels and blew over us. Unlike the fresh air outside, the dank interior gave the wind a disgusting odor of dust and mold.

Xander glanced at Helle. "Which is the deepest tunnel?"

She nodded at a tunnel to our left with a wide mouth. "That one."

Tillit lit his two torches and passed one to me before Helle led us down the winding, twisting tunnel. For once Xander wasn't directly behind our guide, but behind Spiros who followed the pretty Miss Helle.

Darda wrapped her coat closer around herself and shivered. "What a horrible place. Why would anyone, much less a god, wish to be in such chilling caves?"

Helle raised her eyes to the ceiling and swept her gaze over the sparkling stones. "There's a certain charm to the Omorfia Stones. They hold a coldness that soothes the wild winds."

Xander arched an eyebrow. "Omorfia Stones?"

She nodded. "Yes. It means 'beauty,' and I can't think of a more perfect name."

"Where did you hear that name?" Xander persisted.

Helle looked ahead of us and shook her head. "I-I'm not sure."

"Why does that matter?" I spoke up.

Xander turned his head to one side so I could see half of his face. "The name 'Omorfia Stones' is an ancient one. I have only seen it referenced in a very old book in the library of Alexandria." He returned his attention to our young guide. "Where did you hear such an ancient name?"

"I-I must have heard it from one of the sailors," Helle told him.

We entered a large cavern with a ceiling made up of evil-looking stalactites and a floor festooned with sunken smooth stones. Xander planted his feet firmly near the entrance and glared at Helle. "I believe we have been led far enough without the truth."

Helle turned to him and her face was pale. Spiros spun around and frowned at the dragon lord. "To what truth are you referring? What lies have been told?"

Xander's gaze remained fixed on Helle. "You know these caves far better than even the most knowledgeable sailor, you refer to ancient names as though they are native to your tongue, and you plead for the life of one who threatens tens of thousands of lives. With such a list I must demand to know what secret you hide, for you are not who you appear to be."

The young woman shrank back from his accusations. Spiros stepped in front of Helle and faced Xander with anger in his eyes. In all of our travels this was the first time I'd seen him cross with Xander. "You are my lord, but I will not let you slander an innocent woman like this."

Xander's eyebrows crashed down. "Stand aside, captain."

Spiros shook his head. "I will not, My Lord."

Tillit stepped between them and raised his hands so that his torch lit up their tense faces. "Wait a minute here, fellows. Tempers won't help any of us."

"Remain to the side, Tillit!" Xander ordered him.

Darda stood tall and glared at the dragon lord. "My Lord, I despise this sus as well as anyone, but in this instance he does not deserve harsh words." Xander clenched his teeth, but didn't reply.

"She's right," I spoke up as I took a step toward him.

My foot landed on one of those inconspicuous smooth stone and a groaning noise echoed over the cavern. We all froze and swept our eyes over the area.

Helle's eyes widened before they fell on us. "Go back!"

We had half-turned when cracks appeared beneath us and parts of the floor fell away. I stumbled over the uneven ground, and fell onto my hands and knees. The floor completely collapsed beneath me and I fell into the darkness. Xander spun around and leapt in with me while the others were also swallowed.

The drop was fifty feet onto an unforgiving rock floor strewn with pebbles. Fortunately, we had enough dragons to catch all the non-fliers so that everyone landed on their feet, or in my case in the arms of my dragon lord. Unfortunately, we lost our torches and landed in near-complete darkness. Only the faint glow of the bright crystal walls gave us light.

Darda, one arm clutching the bag while another held onto the squirming hand of Tillit, dropped him five feet short of the floor. He landed hard on his rear. Her face was red from the effort as she landed before him breathing hard.

Tillit stood and rubbed his posterior as he glared at her. "You could do with some rescue practice."

She glared at him. "And you could do with a little less weight."

Xander set me down and turned to Helle as she was placed on the floor by Spiros. There was anger in his eyes and a sharpness in his voice. "You told us you knew every floor shaft."

She shook her head. "That wasn't there before. It's been changed."

A low rumble echoed around us. My blood ran cold when I realized it was the sound of someone chuckling.

CHAPTER 30

A cold wind blew around us like a disobedient child as it pulled at our clothes and hair. The shimmering Omorfia Stones grew brighter as an unearthly light swirled before us. It was like a small tornado that formed itself into the familiar figure of Phrixus, god of pains in the ass. It was he who chuckled as he hovered there ten feet above the floor and twenty feet away from us.

"What strange mice I have found in my domain," he commented.

Xander stepped forward to the front of our group and met the eerie gaze of the god. "We have come to offer you one last chance to leave of your own free will."

Phrixus's smile slipped from his lips. "You mortals are as foolish as you are short-lived. I am master of this area, a truth that will continue on long after your race has vanished, even if I must do it myself."

MYTHS BEYOND DRAGONS

Helle stepped up to Xander's side and stared up at the young man with sad eyes. I started back at the physical similarity between the two. My eyes fell on Spiros who stood close to me. His gaze traveled between the two, and I could see a deep pain in them.

Helle looked up at the young man and shook her head. "You can't mean that, Phrixus. They've done nothing to you."

He sneered at her. "You are too kind, sister."

Spiros's eyes widened and he whipped his head to Helle. "Is this true? Did you hide your true identity from us knowing we were looking for your brother and you?" She shrank beneath his accusation.

Darda gasped. "Of course! Helle, sister of Phrixus and goddess of the storms!"

Tillit snorted. "A little late for that bit of info."

Spiros pursed his lips and took a step toward Helle. "Is it true?"

Helle stepped away from Xander and turned to face our small group. She bit her lower lip and gave a small nod. "It's true."

Spiros stood straight and frowned. "I see."

Helle's eyes widened and she shook her head. "I didn't mean to lie to you!" She swept her eyes over all of us. "Any of you! I only wanted to live among you and learn about you-"

"How ironic," Phrixus spoke up as he floated behind his sister and closer to the ground. He leaned his lips close to those of his sister and spoke in a low, tense whisper. "You abandoned me for these worms only to have them reject you."

Tears sprang into her eyes as she gazed at Spiros. He pursed his lips and set a hand on the butt of his weapon. She shut her eyes and turned her face away from him. "I never wanted to hurt anyone."

Phrixus lowered himself to near the floor and lay his hands on her shoulders. "Even if these mortals reject you, *I* still need you, dear sister. I cannot create the End Time Winds without you."

"We do not reject her." We all looked to that most unexpected source, Xander. His steady gaze lay on Helle. "My friends and I would never reject anyone who offers true friendship."

She cringed. "But I've lied to you. I'm not one of you, or even of your world."

"Yes, but you also sought to help us, even at the risk of sending your brother back to your world," he pointed out. He took a step forward and stretched out one hand to her. "You trusted us that we would not send your brother away. Now we will trust you to side with life, mortal or otherwise."

A thin strand of wind that resembled a whip slithered from the shadows and wrapped itself around the wrist of Xander's outstretched arm. It lifted him off the floor and threw him against the far wall.

"Xander!" I shouted as I rushed to his side. I grabbed his shoulders as he sat up.

Phrixus floated higher into the air and stretched out his arm. More of the tendrils of wind wrapped around his limb. "Foolish mortal. You have no idea the power we hold over your lives. However-" his eyes flickered to Helle, "-I would spare these creatures if you would but return to me. Together we will create the End Time Winds and wash these lakes clean of these impurities."

Spiros took a step forward. "Is this what you truly wish, Helle? That so many should suffer?"

She shut her eyes and shook her head. "I couldn't live with myself if something happened to you." She opened her eyes and raised them to him. There were tears in their soft depths as a bitter smile slipped onto her lips. "Iironic, isn't it? That one as old as I should fall in love so quickly."

MYTHS BEYOND DRAGONS

He lowered his weapon hand and smiled at her. "Life is full of ironies, and choices. You have a terrible choice, one that places you between your brother and your friends, between life and death."

She turned to face him and stepped back closer to her brother. "I'm sorry. All I can hope is that I save you and your friends."

"What about Agatha?"

She froze and her eyes widened. Her voice came out in a strangled whisper. "Agatha. . ."

Spiros took a step toward her and held out his hand. "I cannot pretend to know of these End Time Winds or what power you possess, but I know something of your heart. No one capable of such kindness could destroy so many lives."

Phrixus laughed. "Your ignorance is astounding, mortal! My sister is the goddess of storms! She is only destruction!"

She stiffened her upper lip and whipped her head up to her brother. "Stop this at once, Phrixus! I am who I choose to be, and I choose to side with my friends to save everyone!"

Phrixus closed his eyes and shook his head. "Ah, my little sister, how naive you are. You do not understand that these creatures will soon die at their own hand."

"Only if you're the one pushing the sword through us," I quipped.

Phrixus opened his eyes and sneered at me. "Foolish fae-child. Even as we speak an army of little people crosses through a portal and into the dark city, creating havoc with the natural balance of the area and leading not only to their own demise but that of all creatures within and around the lake."

Xander whipped his head up and glared at the god. "Where is this portal?"

Phrixus snorted. "You should be more concerned with your own safety." He returned his attention to Helle and held out his hand to her. "Will you come with me, sister, or must I teach you a harsh lesson about the frailty of mortals?"

Helle glanced from his face to his hand before she looked over to Spiros. She swallowed a lump in her throat and looked back to her brother. "I can't follow you any more, Phrixus." She took a step back closer to Spiros and shook her head. "I'm sorry, but I can't let them die. Even if the portals are their fault, I can't let any of them be hurt."

Phrixus narrowed his eyes and dropped his hand to his side. "You fool. Have you no eyes?"

"She has a sight greater than yours," Spiros spoke up. He stepped up to Helle's side and set a hand on her shoulder. She looked up and he smiled down at her. "She knows compassion and kindness, and in this world there is no better sight than to see through the eyes of another."

Tears appeared in Helle's eyes as she returned his smile with one of her own. "Thank you."

He bowed his head. "It is my pleasure."

Phrixus's eyes widened as he studied the pair. A choked laugh erupted from his throat. "You cannot be serious! What a joke this is, Helle! To love a mortal is to love death!"

Helle whipped her head to her brother and frowned at him. "Then I will love *beyond* death, for not even death can kill love."

A harsh wind whipped out from Phrixus and blasted us with its cold air. Spiros slipped in front of Helle and protected her while my dragon lord covered me. Tillit and Darda fought over the honor before the heavier sus won out and protected her with his body. The wind whipped around us like little cyclones as Phrixus flew upward so he floated among the stalactites and the opening through which we fell.

Phrixus drew back his arm across his chest and glared at his sister. "We will see if death cannot kill your love for this mortal."

Helle's eyes widened. "Phrixus-!"

MYTHS BEYOND DRAGONS

Phrixus swept his arm across his chest, sending a slice of air before him that sheared the bases of the stalactites from the ceiling. The sharp spikes slammed into the ground around us. Xander wrapped his arms around me and rolled us out of the way as the point of a giant one sank into the place where we just vacated. We struggled to our feet as the earth shook beneath us. Clouds of dust covered the Omorfia Stones, sinking the area into greater darkness.

A wind funnel appeared around Phrixus as he half-turned away from us. "Goodbye, sister, and I hope to see you soon."

Helle stretched her hand out to her brother. "Wait! Please save them!"

Phrixus paused and frowned at her. "Remain here and watch your precious mortals perish, or join me on the lake. The choice is yours." He changed into his wind form and slipped through a crack the thickness of paper.

His absence didn't stop the violent attempts on our life. A few of his strands of wind remained and attacked the ceiling. The sides of the opening above us began to break away. It fell in large chunks onto the floor, causing further tremors that loosened more stalactites. Under so much weight and pounding the ground beneath us began to buckle. Holes opened in the floor and swallowed the loose stones like hungry monsters.

Xander glanced at Helle who was held up by Spiros. "Are you able to stop the shaking?" he asked her.

Helle shook her head. "No. Though between us I have the more power, I'm also less able to control my winds. If I were to unleash my powers here the storms would rip you all apart."

Tillit snapped his fingers. "That's why the lake winds aren't as bad as they used to be! You did that!"

She nodded. "Yes. We sought to protect the waters from the fishermen, but when they built those new boats my brother decided they had to be destroyed. I became curious about a creature so ingenious and bold enough to risk my powers to catch fish, so I left him and his ideas, and went into Psychi. When I learned what wonderful people lived in the city I have tried to call to him to convince him of his folly, but he would not reply."

"Less talk, more escape!" I shouted

Darda grabbed Tillit's hand and tugged him toward the center of the room. "We must fly!"

An ominous groan made us all look up. The ceiling in the cavern above us buckled toward us. Tons of bone crushing rock eased toward us.

A strange sound like a whoosh made me look to my left. The winds of the god flew around that area like a hive of bees, and in the middle of their cloister was a large portal. The winds scattered as it widened and sailed across the room, leaving tiny portals in their wake.

My eyes widened. "Oh my god." I whipped my head to Xander. "Phrixus's magic is creating the portals!"

Our stone prison shuddered. The two ceilings above us groaned. Cracks appeared and raced across the surface and down the walls. Another tremor and we would be flattened.

"We must escape through the portals!" Xander yelled over the wind.

"But we do not know to where they lead!" Spiros shouted.

The cave system trembled again. Rocks clattered from the walls and the gentle streams of water became little spouts that shot out and hit the ground, creating fast-growing puddles.

"No, but if we remain here there is only death!" Tillit argued.

A portal appeared in the floor where Darda stood. She screamed as she was swallowed into its black depths. Her hold on Tillit meant she dragged him in with her.

MYTHS BEYOND DRAGONS

I made to follow them, but Xander grabbed my hand. "We have a better chance of warning Psychi if we try different portals," he pointed out.

A portal opened behind Helle and Spiros. The captain glanced at us. "Take care of yourself, My Lord."

Xander smiled and nodded. "The same to you, old friend." His eyes flickered to Helle. "And to you, as well."

She gave him a small smile before the pair vanished into the portal. A final, violent tremor rocked the area. The two ceilings caved in on us. Xander lifted me into his arms and leapt into a nearby portal a second before the rocks crushed it.

CHAPTER 31

I tumbled head-over-heels through the suffocating-but blissfully short-trip through the portal and rolled out the other side. A hard brick wall stopped my tumble as my back slammed into its unforgiving surface so that I ended up upside down with my feet dangling in my face.

Through my feet I could see Xander as he stood up a few feet short of the swirling portal. The black vortex floated near another brick wall like mine, both of which made up the two sides of a wide alley. A few forgotten lobster traps and bits of trash were all that littered the area.

Xander walked over to me and helped me to my feet. "Where are we?" I asked him.

He looked over his shoulder and upward over the top of the buildings. "Zem."

I followed his gaze and my mouth dropped open as I beheld a sheer cliff face that stretched a mile into the sky. The mountain curved to the right so that its rocky wall made up half of the city's border, and all of its gloom as it cast its long shadow over the metropolis.

Still, it was darker than even a shadow could cast. I looked up at the sky and my eyes widened. A huge funnel of wind rose from the center of the upper lake and blotted out the sun with its great weightless girth. The water it carried in its dizzying depths flew up and burst into clouds, blocking the blue sky with black nimbus. In the far distance beyond the cliffs of Chasma I could see another wind funnel swirl in the depths of the lower lake. I swear I could hear the faint echo of the Chasma horn being blown.

I pointed at the huge tornado made of wind and water. "What the hell is that?"

Xander followed my finger and pursed his lips. "If I had to guess I would say that is a part of the End Time Winds the god mentioned."

"And us stuck here. . ." I grumbled.

"That is to our advantage," he argued as he slipped over to the mouth of the alley and glanced around the corner.

I arched an eyebrow. "How?"

"We must also stop the Black dragons from their war, and as the god told us the short army was marching on the other side," he reminded me.

I shook my head. "No, what we need to do is figure out how all those little wind thingies of his were able to make portals."

"That is not surprising, and explains a great deal," he countered.

My mouth dropped to the ground. "What in both our worlds are you talking about? It explains what?"

"Crates warned us that should the gods remain on our plane they would wreak havoc, and the portals may very well be an example of that havoc," he pointed out. "Unfortunately, we must find the portal through which Salome's army passes."

My face fell. "So somewhere around this city is a portal big enough to fit a dwarf and we have to find it."

"Yes."

"That might take a while," I pointed out. I paused and listened. There was nary a sound of cartwheels, horses, or people. I crept over to Xander and lowered my voice to a whisper. "Where is everybody, anyway? This place looks and sounds like a ghost town."

"I have no doubt that under the menace of that funnel a curfew has been enacted," he surmised as he looked around. "Under a curfew no one is allowed on the streets except the guards."

"Great. So no one is going to see us, but if they do we're in big trouble," I guessed.

He nodded. "Yes, though that is the least of our worries."

I arched an eyebrow. "You *do* have a plan for stopping an entire army that's invading *your* enemy's territory, don't you?"

He shook his head. "No, but we may be able to stop them by blocking the opening of the portal."

"And if it works like the others and there's no way to push them back into it?" I reminded him.

He pursed his lips. "Then we will have to stop them however we can."

"What about telling Philip about them and letting him handle things?" I suggested.

Xander shook his head. "If he learned of the invasion that would invariably start a war that might devastate the lakes as greatly as anything Phrixus has promised."

I sighed and ran a hand through my hair. "I was afraid you'd say that. I guess we should start looking for that portal. You want to take the southern haystack or the northern?"

"Since no one has raised the alarm we might guess that the portal is in or near the Windy Caves. They would be the only location where one might hide such a large army," he surmised.

I looked at the mountains in the distance and pursed my lips. "All right, but let me change first." I glanced down at my clothes and changed them into snappy jeans, a black sweater and a nifty black trench coat. "Now we can go."

Xander stretched his neck out and looked both ways before he darted out. I followed him along the alley as it wound its way through the city. We crossed countless larger thoroughfares with roads covered in soft lake stones. A few of the byroads were a little smaller than even the alley, and along their paths I glimpsed small open squares with community wells. We passed by such a road and a dark shadow made me freeze. My eyes widened and my mouth dropped open as the figure raised its head from the water bucket.

It was Kyma, or a good imitation of the old mare, complete with strange markings and a hint of her round scar on her forehead. Her lazy eyes met mine and she licked loose droplets of water from her lips.

I returned my attention to Xander who was a good forty feet ahead of me. "Xander!" I hissed.

He stopped and glanced over his shoulder. "What is it?"

I gestured to him. "Come here and tell me I'm not crazy!"

Xander pursed his lips, but returned to my side. I pointed at the mare. "Is that Kyma?"

He squinted at the old creature before he stiffened and his eyes widened. "By all the gods. . ."

I marched up the street to the old horse and parted the hair on her upper forehead. There, for all the world to see, was the familiar round scar.

Xander came up behind me and shook his head. "I cannot understand how she came to be here."

"Well, however it happened we can't leave her here," I insisted.

Xander pursed his lips as he studied the bare face of the old mare. "It would be impossible to lead her. She has no bridle or reins."

My face fell and I looked back to the trusty steed. "Sorry, old girl, but he's right."

I stroked her nose before Xander and I slipped down the street. We'd gone about ten feet when I heard a clomping behind us. I looked over my shoulder and yelped. Kyma followed a foot behind me so that I nearly bumped into her nose.

I stumbled forward and crashed into Xander who whipped his head around and frowned at me. "What are you-" he looked past me and frowned at the horse. "We cannot have her follow us. She is too large and may be seen."

I turned to face him and put my hands on my hips. "You want to tell the stubborn horse who can travel across two lakes to leave us alone?"

He pursed his lips. "Very well, she may come, but try to keep her close."

My eyes flickered to the horse and I snorted. "I don't think that'll be a problem. . ."

Together the three of us crept down the streets. We'd gone two blocks when Xander pushed me against the outer wall of a building and pressed his own back against the stone. We were stopped at the corner and in front of us was a narrow street. Four shadows appeared on the ground and grew larger before the owners appeared. They were four young men dressed in black armor. At their hips were white swords with black hilts. Their keen eyes searched the area, but the darkness hid us in its thick cloak.

All of us except for Kyma. One of the guards jerked to a stop and grabbed the hilt of his sword as he glared in our direction. "Who goes there? Come out where we can see you!"

MYTHS BEYOND DRAGONS

I glanced over my shoulder at the horse. The color drained from my face when I saw that Kyma's ample behind stuck out from the wall as her face nuzzled against my shoulder.

"Come out!" he demanded again as he and his comrades drew their weapons.

I looked up at Xander. "What now?"

Xander pursed his lips. "Follow my lead." He stepped out of the shadows, but I grabbed his arm.

Xander looked over his shoulder at me and I smiled and winked at him. "How about you follow my lead?"

I slipped around him and into the open where I held up my hands. "Hey, boys. Mind telling me how to get to the nearest bar?"

"State your business here," the lead guard demanded.

Xander stepped out after me with his hands raised. "We are merely travelers through the city."

The leader of the guards scoffed. "Travelers who lurk in the darkness?"

"Magicians, actually," I spoke up as I lowered my arms. The men tensed. I lucked my tongue and shook my head. "There's no need to do that. I just wanted to show you a little trick with my clothes." My eyes flickered to Xander. "On three. One, two, *three*!"

I changed my clothes to a startling neon-pink color that would have blinded a blind man. The guards started back and gaped at the change. Xander leapt at them and knocked two of their helmeted heads together before the other pair recovered. He drew out Bucephalus and made quick work of them,

I reverted my clothes back to black and Xander sheathed his weapon. Kyma strode up to me and nuzzled her face against my shoulder. I patted her on the nose. "It's okay. You didn't mean to."

Xander stiffened and whipped his head down the street. Shouts came from that direction.

He grabbed my hand and pulled me onto a side street with Kyma close behind. "We must hurry."

"You! Halt!" a voice shouted behind us.

Yeah, that wasn't happening.

CHAPTER 32

Somehow the old mare was able to keep up with our sprint as we made a mad dash to the Windy Caves. The city erupted in a cacophony of gongs that vibrated the air. More shouts came from behind us. I glanced over my shoulder to see a dozen black-clad guards racing after us.

"We're leading a lot of people right to the caves!" I shouted at Xander.

"We have no choice!" he countered.

I couldn't argue with that, not when another half dozen sprouted from the side streets not more than a half block from us. We reached the outskirts of the city with dozens of city guards at our backs. The buildings parted and in their places was a large system of corrals in which were stocked a countless number of pani. The ground sloped down to those pens, and beyond them was the foreboding foothills of the Heavy Mountains. The Windy Caves dotted the hillside as they had on the north side of the lower lake.

We had only a hundred yards between us and those caves, but Xander stopped us and frowned.

At the bottom of that slope stood a familiar face: Philip Keper. On either side of him stood a hundred armed guards, and on his face was a sly smile. He beckoned to us. We couldn't argue as our pursuers caught up to us and surrounded our group a couple dozen deep. Xander held his head high as he led Kyma and me down the slope to our 'host.'

We reached Philip and he bowed his head to us. "It is a pleasure to see you again, Lord Xander. To what do we owe this pleasure?"

"War," Xander replied.

Philip lifted his head and arched an eyebrow. "Then you have come to your senses and wish to grant me an alliance with your formidable army?"

Xander shook his head. "No. We have come to stop one. Even now your cousin may be amassing her forces at your gates."

Philip chuckled. "That would be quite a feat. Either her dwarves have learned to climb without being seen or they have learned to breath under water."

"Neither. They have found a portal which is bringing them here," Xander explained.

"What a fantastic story, but one better suited to fiction," our 'host' scoffed.

Xander nodded at the Windy Caves. "Search those caves. I have no doubt you fill find the army hidden in their depths."

"I would rather my men search you-" he leaned to one side and smiled at me, "-and your lovely Maiden while you explain how you came to be in my city without anyone noticing."

"It's not that hard when everyone's hiding from that funnel," I quipped.

MYTHS BEYOND DRAGONS

He frowned at me. "Yes, there's that trouble, as well. The wind funnel appeared less than a half hour before the alarm was raised about you." His eyes flickered to Xander. "You wouldn't happen to know anything about that wind, would you?"

"Your priorities should be in stopping the war that is about to engulf your city," Xander persisted.

Anger flashed in Philip's eyes. "That is enough. I will hear no more of-"

"My Lord!" one of the men behind us and up the slope shouted. Everyone turned to him and he pointed at the foothills. "The Caves!"

We followed his finger and watched as torches were lit in the entrances of the Windy Caves. The torches were held up by an army of dwarves, Salome's army. The brightest flame was located in the center where stood a large cave entrance. Silhouetted against the flickering flames of dozens of torches stood Salome. Even from this distance I could see the wide grin on her lips.

"What do you think of my army, cousin?" she called to Philip.

Philip turned to face her and his army surrounded him. "I believe you are short a victory, cousin."

Salome laughed. "What a wit you are, cousin, but my army will show you the true power of a dwarven ax."

She turned her head and gave a nod. The dwarves lifted their axes and gave a wild cry before they cascaded out of the caves. Salome herself leapt into the air and transformed into her full dragon self complete with wicked tail and ugly head.

Philip lifted his fist in the air. "For Zem!"

"For Zem!" shouted his men as they raced past us and toward the corrals. Philip, too, transformed into his full dragon shape and flew into the sky. The generals clashed before their armies had gone half their distance.

I looked up at Xander. His face was pale as his gaze lay on the coming battle. "Well? Are you waiting for an invitation? Go and stop them!"

He shook his head. "Not all the Sæ within me could stop this battle. Both armies see themselves as fighting for their people, and in such an important matter no one will be halted."

Tears sprang into my eyes as I balled my hands into fists at my sides. "We can't just stand here and watch!"

"There is nothing that can be done."

I stood straight and swallowed the lump in my throat. "I'm going to try."

I took a step forward, but a large body passed me in a quick lope. It was Kyma, and she was headed straight for the battle.

I stretched my hand out, but missed her tale by an inch. "Kyma! Come back here, you dumb horse!"

Kyma raced for the corral gate and crashed through what Philip's army had climbed over. The pani parted at her coming and made a wide path down which she traveled. She lifted her head to the dark sky and let loose a whinny that echoed off the mountain walls.

The pani lifted their heads and bleated in return before they moved as a swell toward the converging armies. It was a sight to watch tens of thousands of horned sheep move as one toward the center of the maze of corrals. They were stopped by dozens of fences, but with their girth they pushed them over and trampled them into the ground. The earth shook beneath us as their countless hooves trod into position.

The armies didn't notice the flanking maneuvers of the cattle creatures until they were surrounded on all sides and separated from their companions. The dragons tried to wade through, but the pani bit at their ankles and head-butted them back into their place. Some of the dwarves swung their axes at the beasts, but they were jumped from behind and, with a horrible scream, disappeared beneath the white wool. A few of those disappearances stopped any further struggles on behalf of the drwarven army.

The whole process only took a minute and no one on the ground was spared save for Xander and me. Kyma stood in the center of her vast herds of pani and turned to me. I swear her long mouth was smiling at me.

I turned my wide eyes to my dragon lord. He, too, looked dumbfounded. "What did we just see?" I asked him.

He snapped his open mouth shut and shook his head. "I cannot hope to fathom it."

The armies were out of the way, but that left the generals. They were locked in aerial combat above our heads as each tried to tear the other apart. The pair let loose their terrible dragon breath and scorched the skies. Some of those flames fell on the trapped armies and caused beast and person to scatter. Other flame balls shots flew over the city and crashed into streets and buildings. The gongs sounded again as the air filled with the sounds of people screaming.

Xander stepped forward with his gaze ever on the fighting dragon kin and pursed his lips. "Remain here."

I grabbed his arm and gave a nice, hard tug. "Now wait a second here! It's one thing to fight some small armies or a single Red Dragon, but we're talking about *two* wannabe dragon lords here. If one doesn't tear you to shreds the other might sneak up behind you and finish you off!"

Xander turned to me and clasped my hands in his as he smiled down at me. "Do you remember at Alexandria where you told me I should not doubt myself?"

"Yeah, but you weren't supposed to try to get yourself killed with my advice!" I snapped.

He chuckled as he stepped backward away from me. "How could I allow myself to die when I have such a lovely Maiden to return to?"

I tried to hold onto his hands, but Xander slipped from my grasp and turned away to take a few steps. I tried to grab him, but he unfurled his thick, long wings. Their appearance made me stumble back to avoid being pushed around by them.

Xander glanced over his shoulder and smiled at us. His eyes were bright green. "Protect the city as best you can by putting out the fires. I will return as soon as I can."

He hunkered down before he leapt into the air. A blast of wind blew over us and scattered dust over me so that I was forced to shut my eyes. When I opened them again Xander was high in the air. He flew straight up, and as he flew his body changed to that of his full dragon form.

My heart beat faster as he grew to enormous size, far larger than any of the two dragons who fought one another. His girth was not as great as that of the mad Red Dragon, but it did remind me of the time in the Sæ pool where he'd tried to make me into a dragon snack.

My eyebrows crashed down and I balled my hands into fists at my side. "Come on, Miriam, get a grip on yourself because you *know* he's got a grip on himself."

Xander reached the same height as the battling pair and, with the grace of an elegant serpent, flew toward them. He opened his great mouth and deep in the depths appeared the bright orange fire of his breath. He opened fire on the pair, pelting both of them with hot spitballs that knocked them apart and left them scorched.

The pair of dragons spun around and turned their collective fury on Xander. They shot fireballs and long trails of flame at him. Xander dodged the fireballs and used his thick wings to block the flamethrower barrage.

Unfortunately, their fire battle fell on the city. The residents were doing their best to put out the flames, but they were dragons, not firefighters. I took a deep breath before I raced into the city. I retraced Xander and my steps to one of the many wells we had passed. Men, women, and children stood in long lines and passed buckets between them to fill with water and douse the flames.

MYTHS BEYOND DRAGONS

"Coming through!" I yelled as I pushed my way to the low stone wall that surrounded the well.

I raised both my hands and from the depths of the well came my tall columns of water dragons. The citizens gasped and stumbled back. Many fell backwards and gaped up at my dragons as they towered over the square.

I pointed at the fires that surrounded us. "Go get 'em, boys!"

The dragons roared and plunged into the fires. Steam rose from their bodies, but they were replenished by the deep well source so that they never shrank. In a matter of minutes they had succeeded in extinguishing the fires within a couple of blocks. Unfortunately, there were fires all across the wide city.

"Come on, boys, let's take a trip into the city!" I called to my water pets.

I raised my hands higher, but my dragons didn't increase in length. However, the sounds of far-off screams did make me look deeper into the city. My eyes widened as I beheld another two dozen of my water dragons that towered above the buildings. Thy had come from all the other wells in the city, and together they unleashed a roar that shook the very ground.

I blinked at the dragons as they threw themselves atop the many fires. "Wow. . ." I whispered.

Sweat appeared on my brow as the pressure to maintain so many large water dragons began to drain my energy. I looked up at the skies. Xander was still in combat with the other two dragons, but they were like lumbering elephants compared to his quick movements.

"Come on, Xander. Hurry it up. . ." I muttered as my arms began to shake.

My pets extinguished so many fires that a soft mist fell over the city, smothering any new flames that the fighting dragons cast to the earth.

The dragons broke off their attack and faced each other with Xander opposing the other two. They roared at him and flew at him. Xander spun around and smacked Philip, the larger of his two foes, in the face. He crashed down to the ground near the corrals and lay still among a thin cloud of dust.

Salome tried to wrap her lithe body around Xander's neck, but he snapped his jaws over her thin form and shook her like she was a chew toy. She cried out in terror and he released her. Her wings were too damaged by Xander's rough treatment to hold her up and she, too, fell to the earth like a shooting star.

That was one problem down and one very windy problem left.

CHAPTER 33

My dragon lord flew triumphant over the skies. He swept past me and roared his glee. The citizens trembled at the might of a dragon capable of defeating two claimants to the throne. I frowned as I glimpsed a little too much blood lust in those green eyes of his.

"Time to come down from your perch," I snapped as I stretched out my arms and clapped my hands together.

All my dragons but my two closest disappeared, and the pair that remained combined to make a giant one. The next time Xander paraded past me my dragon flew up and slapped its body across his face. He fluttered back and shook his head. The evil light in his eyes disappeared, and he glanced down.

I gave a tiny wave before I dropped my limb to my side. My arm felt like a heavy log, as did my legs. Xander flew down to my square and transformed back into his human self a yard away from me.

A smile was on his lips as he stepped up to me and grasped my shoulders. "Thank you for that slap. I was in need of such a scolding."

"My. . .my pleasure," I gasped. If he hadn't been holding me I wouldn't have been standing.

I heard a soft murmur and glanced around. The citizens had us surrounded. Their clothes were of the plainest gray, but were well kept. They were covered in the grime from their firefighting, but were otherwise clean. They kept a perimeter of ten feet away from us and gaped at Xander and me.

Xander set me on the top of the well wall and turned to the growing crowd. "Citizens of Zem, I am Lord Xander Alexandros of Psychi. I am sorry I-"

One of the men raised his arm in the air. "Three cheers for Lord Xander!"

Dozens of others raised their hands in the air. "Hip-hip-hooray! Hip-hip-hooray! Hip-hip-hooray!"

Xander smiled and bowed his head. "My Maiden and I were happy to be of service to you."

A harsh wind blew over us and made the crowd duck against its cold touch. Xander and I looked in the direction of the lake. The funnel spun faster than before and its width increased with each rotation. Little wisps of wind stretched out like tendrils and raced through the city, opening portals wherever they went.

Xander scooped me into his arms and leapt into the air. His wide wings spread out on either side of him and we sailed through the wild skies. It was like sailing on rough seas as each tendril and blast of wind tried to rock us and knock us to the earth. The portals also didn't help as they sprang out of nowhere in our path and around us. Xander had a hard time dodging the many obstacles, so I tightly wrapped my arms around his neck and squeezed myself against his chest.

MYTHS BEYOND DRAGONS

I looked up into Xander's tense face as we approached the funnel. "Any idea how to stop these things?"

He shook his head. "No, but Helle may be able to assist us."

My face fell before I looked out on the storm ahead of us. "If we can find her."

One of the popping portals appeared five feet ahead of us. Xander didn't have a chance to dodge before we were tumbling through the suffocating darkness. He didn't lose his grip on me and we came out of the portal back-first so that he landed on his back on a row of hard planks and I landed on him.

A chuckle made me tilt my head back and look behind us. Xander and I lay on one of the larger of the Psychi port battleship docks. Behind us stood our friends, Darda, Tillit, Spiros, and Helle. At their backs was a city in slightly-controlled chaos as people hurried from their homes and away from the lake, taking with them whatever they could carry.

Of our friends it was the sus who chuckled at us. "You always seem to come out on top of your lord, Miriam."

Darda helped me up while Spiros lent a hand to Xander. The dragon lord turned his attention to his captain. "What is the situation?"

Spiros nodded at the lake where dozens of portals swirled between the docks on the funnel. "The military vessels would be useless on such unpredictable waters, so all the resources have been put into evacuating the citizens."

I looked to Helle who's pained face was turned to the funnel. "Is this the End Time Winds?"

She nodded. "Yes."

"How exactly are they to destroy the cities?" Xander asked her.

She nodded at the funnel. "Those wind tunnels are designed to pull the cities off the ground and drown everything in the lake."

"Why does he hesitate to attack?" Darda wondered.

Helle stepped to the front of our group and pursed her lips as she studied the huge wind-and-water tornadoes. "It isn't that he's hesitating, it's that without my powers it takes him three times as long to build up enough wind to tear the very foundations of the cities from the ground."

"Then we still have a chance to stop him," Darda commented.

Tillit snorted. "Not likely. First, we have to find the little ass, and then we have to figure out how to stop him."

"I know where he is," Helle told him.

"That still leaves the defeating part," he persisted.

Xander looked to Helle. "You told us your powers were greater, but that you had little control over them. Can you stop him?"

She shrank back and shook her head. "I-I can't. I might destroy the cities."

"Then you realize we have no choice but to return him to your realm with the Theos Chime," Xander pointed out as his eyes flickered to the bag that Darda held in which the Chime box was hidden.

The color drained from her face. She grasped Xander's arm and shook her head. "You can't do that! He might never be able to come back!"

His expression softened as he looked into her eyes. "Would we have another choice I would certainly accept that option, but your brother is intent on destroying many innocents. Knowing his determination, would you still refuse us this final chance?"

Helle's face fell as she dropped her arms to her side and lowered her eyes to the ground. "No. . ."

Xander set a hand on her shoulder. "We will try one last time, and then-" She shut her eyes, but nodded.

"But where is he?" Darda spoke up.

MYTHS BEYOND DRAGONS

Helle sniffled and raised her tear-pooling eyes to the point where the two bodies of water met. "There. The Chasma. He means to watch both destructions."

Spiros raised his gaze to the wild air above us. "The winds make it impossible to fly."

Darda turned to me and smiled. "Your water dragons could take us."

The mere thought of using my powers made my legs quiver. I shook my head. "After putting out dozens of fires in Zem I don't think I've got it in me right now."

Tillit puffed out his chest. "Which is where I come in."

Darda glanced at him and narrowed her eyes. "How can *you* get us there?"

He grinned and tapped the side of his ample schnoz. "With this, my dear Darda. Give me a fast ship and a little help from our captain here-" he gestured to the surprised Spiros, "-and we'll make it there in no time."

Spiros shook his head. "I am a captain of men, not of ships."

"But you've still got the Zoi map, right?" Tillit asked him.

Darda rolled her eyes. "The map is useless in finding the portals."

"That's where the old sniffer comes in," he told her as he opened his bag at his hip and rummaged through the vast contents. "What you humans, dragons, and even goddesses haven't figured out is these portals aren't like the natural ones. Those natural ones smell like wild roses on a warm summer day. These ones smell like my grandmother's toes, or-" he pulled out a wrinkled brown cap mushroom, "-like rotten truffles, a sus's favorite treat when they aren't rotten."

I clapped my hand over my nose as a pungent odor hit my nostrils. "Please tell me we're not taking that with us."

Tillit looked to Spiros. "The map, if you please, captain."

Spiros drew out the map and together our group held the ends so it didn't fly away. Tillit stepped up to one of the longer sides and smeared the cap end of the mushroom over the map.

Darda's eyes widened as she watched the sacrilege. "What in all the worlds are you doing?"

Tillit tucked the remains of the mushroom back into his bag and tapped a finger against his lips. "A little patience, my dear Darda. If my all-night study of this map is correct, a little bit of this-" he drew back and cleared his throat. With the speed of a bullet he whipped forward and hocked a loogie on the bits of mushroom.

"You monster!" she shrieked. She whipped her head up from the dripping wet area and glared at him. "Have you no decency? Have you no-"

"Look," he told her as he nodded at the mix of phlegm and rotten mushroom.

Tillit had expertly smeared his mucus and the stinking vegetable over the area of the map that represented the lake. The map glowed a bright yellow color and absorbed the bits of disgusting animal and vegetable into its canvas-like surface.

Tillit looked to Spiros and gestured to the map. "If you would touch the lake, captain."

Spiros stepped up to the map and pressed his hand on the surface. The lake came up as before, but now the portals were shown. There were dozens of them, big and small, and more appearing all the time.

Darda blinked at the floating, enlarged image before she looked to Tillit. "What in all the worlds did you do?"

MYTHS BEYOND DRAGONS

    Tillit puffed out his ample chest and grinned. "A little bit of my own magic, my dear Darda. Some sus nose talent and the scent of those portals, and the map is now better than eyes at seeing the portals." He pushed the map toward Spiros and smiled. "Now's your time to shine for your lady friend, captain." Spiros took the map and folded it before he gave a nod.

    We were ready for anything, or so we hoped.

CHAPTER 34

We commandeered a small boat large enough to hold us, but without ample seating so that half of us were forced to sit on the bottom. With Tillit at the helm and Spiros at his side we set off into the white-capped lake that was spotted with black swirling portals. Our travel was like a game of tag where the portals were 'it' and we had to do our best to avoid the ones that sprouted around us.

"Starboard ten feet!" Spiros shouted.

"Aye aye!" Tillit replied as he pulled on the sail ropes and turned the rudder.

We jerked to the left, and a second later a large portal appeared to our right and a foot off the bow. We sailed past at a distance close enough to touch the edges of the portal.

Darda and I clutched onto the port side as we were thrown hither and thither. Xander kept his position at the bow while Helle leaned over one side and squinted into the distance. The waves grew particularly rough as we bypassed the terrible wind funnel. The wind tore at our sails and whipped my hair against my face, but our helmsman got us around the storm.

Our indirect route meant the trip took longer than it could have, and as we sailed across the rough lake the funnels grew larger. The clouds that blocked the sky thundered and lightning flashed across them. A charge filled the air and made the hair on my arms stand on end.

I glanced at Helle. "So what kind of tricks does your brother know that we need to worry about?"

"He's capable of creating blades from the wind, and there are his wind tendrils which he can use to grab you," she admitted.

I nodded at the funnel closest to us. "And then there's those. How can those to go away?"

"We must break his concentration or render him unconscious, but that will be no mean feat," she warned me.

"I think I'm up for that concentration task," Tillit spoke up.

"Unfortunately, you are a master," Darda agreed.

Helle shook her head. "You don't understand. Because my brother has always had less power he made up for it by learning to focus what he little he possessed, therefore breaking his concentration won't be easy."

"We must try," Xander mused as he looked up at the towering rocks that made up the Chasma.

We were a hundred yards from the Chasma when Darda pointed at the rock walls that climbed up to the edge of the rocky flat where Omonoia stood. "Up there!"

I followed her finger and glimpsed the familiar figure of Phrixus. He floated down from the center of the Chasma to within thirty feet of us. His hard eyes swept over our group and stopped on Helle. "Have you finally come to your senses, sister, and have come to join me in destroying these worthless creatures?"

Helle stood and shook her head. "No, Phrixus, I've come to stop you."

His eyes flickered to Spiros who sat behind her at the helm. A sneer curled over his lips. "I see. In that case I have no choice."

He drew his arm across his chest and large tendrils of wind flew out. They slipped around Helle and pulled her from the boat.

"Helle!" Spiros shouted as he threw aside the map and leapt into the air. His wings unfurled as he drew out his sword.

Phrixus's face lit up with uncontrollable rage. "*You will not interfere, mortal!*"

His other hand shot out, and from his palm flew a long sickle-like blade made of wind. The wind blade sliced across the front of his chest. Spiros's mouth opened in a silent scream as he dropped back-first into the savage waves.

Helle twisted around and her eyes widened as she watched Spiros disappear beneath the white caps. "No!"

Phrixus sneered at the spot where Spiros had fallen. "Now perhaps you will see the light, dear sister."

Helle saw the light, but not the one he was meaning. She whipped her head around and a white light blasted out of her body, cutting her free from her bonds. The brilliance that surrounded her kept her alight as she spread her arms out on either side of her. More, brighter light appeared in her palms, and it was only then that I realized there wasn't any light at all. What surrounded her were winds that defied gravity so much that all I glimpsed was the bright echoes of their travel around her.

Phrixus's eyes widened and he flew back a few yards. "Helle, you cannot mean to-" She threw her light, both hands, at him. Small wind blades with glistening points shot at him. They stabbed him in the limbs and threw him back in an arch that forced him down into the water.

MYTHS BEYOND DRAGONS

Helle turned away from her brother and threw herself into the water where Spiros had gone. Xander, Darda, and I raced to the side of the boat and looked over the edge.

"Watch the rocking!" Tillit scolded us as the ship lurched violently to starboard.

"Can anyone see anything?" I asked my companions.

Darda pursed her lips and shook her head. "Nothing-wait!" She stabbed a finger at the water. "There!"

Air bubbles broke through the surface and were quickly followed by a column of wind that burst upward. A cyclone of wind blew out of the water and landed with a hard slam into the rear of our boat between Tillit and Darda. The winds subsided and revealed Helle. Before her, spread out over the bottom of the boat, lay Spiros. His face was as pale as death and his shirt was sliced open. Blood covered his clothes but couldn't hide the horrible gash that ran across his chest in a perfect line over his scar.

Helle grasped the front of his ruined clothes as tears streamed down her cheeks. "Spiros. . .please, Spiros, don't leave me. Please don't leave me."

Xander pushed past us and moved to Spiros's side opposite Helle. He gently drew her hands away and opened his clothes wider to assess the wound. His face fell.

Helle looked up at the dragon lord with pleading eyes. "Can he be saved?"

Xander drew back and shook his head. "No. There is too much blood loss."

A sob escaped her lips and she draped herself over his chest. Her hands clutched his chest as she cried into his clothes. "No. My people, please don't let this happen. Not to him."

Another bubble of water far from the boat caught my attention. A second later another cyclone flew out of the lake.

"Helle!" came the banshee-like screech of Phrixus as his cyclone burst outward, drenching us with water.

Helle raised her head, but her gaze remained fixed on Spiros's white face. She cupped one of his cheeks in her hand and a bitter smile slipped onto her lips. "My love, my mortal. I would trade the worlds-I would trade anything to be with you in death."

"Miriam!" Darda yelped.

We all looked to her. Through all the chaos and rough seas she still had the bag clutched to her chest. Through the thick canvas we could see a warm glow of light.

I scooted over to her and opened the tough, wet strings that bound the opening. The bag fell away onto Darda's lap and revealed the box in which was held the chime. The light came from inside the box. I tilted the lid open and revealed the glowing brilliance of the Theos Chime.

My eyes flickered up to Helle and then Xander. "You think it's working?"

He shook his head. "I cannot guess."

I returned my attention to the bell and sighed. "Well, here goes."

I grasped the sides of the bell and a warm thrill ran through my body. A line of brilliant yellow light shot out of the bell and struck Helle. She arched her back and her mouth opened in a soundless cry as the light enveloped her. The light pulsed with life and a single strand of flickering brilliance floated out of her and slipped over Spiros's blood-covered body. The light turned a complete circle over his chest before it dove into his wound. His eyes flew open and he arched his back as the light burst out from his body.

Helle struggled through the lethargy the light caused her and grasped one of his hands. The light around both of them combined in a shock wave that blew over us, knocking us to the bottom of the boat. The bell tumbled from my hands and rolled to a stop at Xander's feet. The lights around the bell and the couple vanished, plunging us back into the darkness of the funnels.

MYTHS BEYOND DRAGONS

Helle's eyes rolled back and she slumped over Spiros. The captain's glazed eyes became focused and he weakly looked around. "What. . .what happened?" He glanced down at his chest and his eyes widened. "Helle!"

Spiros tried to sit up, but a sharp cry escaped his lips and he clutched his chest above her. He looked down at himself and froze when he saw the blood that covered his cloths and now his hand.

He raised his hand and gaped at the blood. "I. . .I live?"

Xander smiled down at him. "Yes, and I believe you have this young woman-" he nodded at Helle, "-to thank."

With Xander's help Spiros sat up. The captain drew her into his arms, and I could see she was still breathing. He gave her a gentle shake. "Helle. Helle?"

Her eyes fluttered open and looked at up at him. They widened and a smile spread across her lips. "You're alive!" she shouted as she threw her arms around his neck.

Spiros returned the hug and petted her hair. "Somehow you saved me."

Helle drew back and looked him over as she shook her head. "But I don't understand. My powers don't save people. They-" She raised her hands with the palms up and her eyes widened. "My powers! They're gone!"

Spiros blinked at her. "You are sure?"

She nodded. "Yes! I can't create any wind! Watch!" She thrust one hand out and a tiny breeze of white wind flew out of her palm.

I picked up the bell from the floor of the boat and held it up. The inscription on the inside caught my attention. I wrinkled my brow as I looked over the unfamiliar characters. "I think the words in the bell changed."

"Let me see it," Tillit requested. The chime was passed to the back where he tilted it up and arched an eyebrow. "It *has* changed. Listen." He cleared his throat and read the new rhyme aloud.

*Two are joined
By Mortal fate
Not even Death
Can separate*

Helle's eyes widened. "I'm. .. I'm mortal?"

Spiros's face fell as he studied hers. "Do you regret your choice?"

She looked up at him and shook her head. "No, but-well-" she paused when she noticed his crestfallen face and a smile slipped onto her lips. She reached up and cupped one of his cheeks in her hand. "I regret nothing."

Spiros leaned into her grasp, and his shifting gave me a good look at his chest. I saw the wound was not only healed, but the flesh was healthy. "Your scar is gone!" I spoke up.

Spiros grasped Helle's hands and smiled down at her. "Love heals all wounds."

CHAPTER 35

Love may have healed Spiros's wounds, but it didn't help the boiling temper that bubbled to the surface twenty yards off the starboard. A small hurricane burst up from the surface and a hundred feet into the air before it blasted away, showering us with cold water. Where the hurricane stood now floated Phrixus, and his red face and eyes showed he wasn't happy.

He clenched his hands by his sides and glared at his sister. "How *dare* you touch me!"

Helle climbed to her feet and turned to face her brother. "I dare because I care about these people. *My* people."

Phrixus sneered at her. "They are not like us."

She nodded. "That is true, they can never be gods, but we can be like them." She stood tall and lifted her chin in the air. "*I* am one of them."

Phrixus's eyes widened as the full horror of her words hit him. His mouth flopped open and shut like a fish before he shook himself. "You. . .you cannot be serious. There is no way to revoke the power of a god."

Darda took the box that contained the Theos Chime and held it up to him. "There is now."

Phrixus's eyebrows crashed down and his body trembled. "You. . .you *monsters! What have you done to her?*"

Helle shook her head. "They did nothing. The Theos Chime granted me my wish."

The wind picked up around Phrixus and four thick water spouts, beckoned by the wind, rose from the water to surround him. "You fool! You stupid, ignorant, naive-" One of the water spouts made a sharp bend and hit him in the side of the face.

He flew back at the impact as I waved at him with my raised hand. "You know, you shouldn't play with water around a Mare fae. This happens."

I lifted both my hands and clapped them together. Two of the spouts slammed into either side of him, giving his ears a harsh ring that vibrated his body. I directed the last one to smack him straight in the face so that he was shoved backward ten feet. With the spouts used up I summoned a dozen large water dragons that sprouted up from the water that surrounded the ship.

Phrixus wiped the water from his face and glared at me. "Foolish mortal! Let us see how well you manage without your precious water!"

He lifted his arms high above his head. A hurricane dropped from the black cloud and touched down just in front of him. The rough winds drew the water from the lake and into its depths. My dragons big and small were sucked up into that voracious windstorm and returned to their watery selves as they merged inside the hurricane.

MYTHS BEYOND DRAGONS

The swirling winds drew away from us, taking the water with it as it headed for the nearest funnel. The hurricane left in its wake a muddy lake bottom devoid of all water and life. The tiniest fish and the smallest droplets were gone, taken in its spinning mouths and dragged away. I felt like a piece of myself was drawn away with it.

My companions and I let out cries of fear as our boat plunged a hundred feet down into the mud and sank a foot into the soft ground. Tillit fell backwards over the stern and Darda fell over the starboard, and both became stuck in the mud.

Phrixus lowered himself so he hovered only a few feet above the muddy lake bottom. He folded his arms over his chest and grinned at me. "What will you do now, Mare fae? Your strength has been sent away by my winds to feed the funnel." He half-turned and gestured at his hurricane as it was absorbed into the funnel. "In a few short minutes I shall loose the End Time Winds upon both cities."

I balled my hands into fists at my side and glared at him. "You think you're all that with your wind, don't you?"

Phrixus chuckled. "I am 'all that,' as you say, for I cannot be separated from my strength as you, nor will I make such a fool of myself as he-" he gestured to Xander, "-has done."

Helle regained her proud footing and glared at him. "Phrixus, you fool! You have no idea what you're doing!"

He sneered at her. You are dead to me, my sister. As surely as death will take you, so will I take this city that seduced you into that mortal coil."

Xander stepped forward to the edge of the boat. "She is right, you have no idea what damage you are causing this area." He gestured to the near-empty lake with its hovering portals. "Those portals are not the doing of any human or dragon, but of your powers. You taint this world with your unnatural powers and create these portals that slowly injure the area you profess to love so much."

"Lies!" Phrixus shouted. "I will listen to your lies no more!"

He raised both hands. The funnels spun faster and moved away from us, each toward their own city. The winds at the edge of the monster hurricanes clawed at the port of Psychi and sucked up ships that had been loosened from their moorings and floated some fifty yards off the docks. They were drawn into the center and their planks were torn into bits. Another minute and the same would happen to all of the city.

I bit my lower lip and tried to think of something-anything-that would help us. Then I remembered something Phrixus had said, about being separated from my strength, and a sly smile slipped onto my lips.

"Hey, Phrixus!" I yelled

He returned his attention to me and sneered. "What do you want, mortal?"

I drew my hand back like a baseball pitcher and felt my clothes shift around me. Part of it formed inside my hand as I grinned at Phrixus. "Batter up!"

A puzzled expression appeared on his face as I threw my super-duper, hail-Mary-wet-loogie curve ball at him. From my hand exploded a water dragon, one twice the size as those I used on the Red Dragon. The beast of liquid opened its mouth, a cavernous trap large enough to fit two dozen naqia and still have room for a few pani. I gaped in amazement at the creature I had created as it rose a hundred feet into the air. Its shadow stretched across the muddy plain and the god. Phrixus's face contorted with fear and surprise as he threw up his arms in front of him.

The dragon swallowed him whole and clamped its teeth shut. At the same time the funnels stopped their horrible journey and the winds at the edges slowed.

For a moment all was silent. Then the dragon paused and narrowed its green eyes. Through our joined connection I felt something shift inside its body. The flesh on the back of its neck stretched outward like putty, and in a moment its watery flesh broke open.

The dragon screamed and I clutched my chest as its pain descended to me. It felt like someone had stretched the flesh on my back and snapped it back into place. I fell to one knee and clutched the back of my neck, but I looked up in time to see Phrixus fly fifty feet away and spin around to face us. His body and clothes were soaked, and he had to flip some of his wet hair out of his face to properly glare at my pet and me.

Phrixus balled his hands into fists at his sides as his body trembled. The wind around him cut the air like long daggers. "You water witch! You dare do this to me?"

I climbed to my shaky feet as both my dragon and I turned to face him. "Yeah, we dare."

"Miriam!" Helle shouted. I glanced over my shoulder at her. She pointed at the ground beneath her brother. "The ground is his weakness! You must bring him to the earth!"

I grinned and gave her a thumbs up. "No problem."

"Traitor!" Phrixus screamed.

He stabbed a finger in Helle's direction and his razor-sharp winds flew at her. My water dragon flew in the path of the wind and wrapped its body around the wind blade, but its body only slowed the wind weapon as it flew through the dragon and toward Helle. Spiros wrapped his arms around her and pressed her to his chest before he turned his back to face the blow.

A figure flew past me and stopped in front of the pair. That figure was my dragon lord. He held up the broad side of Bucephalus so that the wind slammed into the shining metal. There was a loud clang and Xander was pushed back a foot, but the wind blade shattered like glass and joined the rest of the air. Phrixus gaped at where his wind had disappeared.

Xander held up his sword and smiled. "You have lost, Phrixus. Crates of Mallus informed me my sword could protect anyone you threaten, and I will guarantee his word is kept."

Phrixus threw back his head and screamed to the air. "Traitors! Everyone!"

While he had his fit my dragon slipped around him like a snake. He hardly had time to gasp before my pet slammed him into the deep mud. The god came up from the ooze looking like a muck monster. My dragon drew back and we watched him flail about with his body dripping with mud. He stumbled toward us, his bright blue eyes glowing against the brown mud.

"Miriam!" Tillit shouted from his own place in the muck. He tossed the bell to me and smiled. "Send this monster to where he belongs."

I hugged the bell to my chest and glanced at Helle. She stiffened her upper lip and nodded at me. I smiled and stood in the boat.

Phrixus's eyes widened as he beheld the Theos Chime in my hands. "No! *No!*"

I grasped the thick wooden handle in one hand and rang it. A loud, clear ding-dong echoed over the whole of the lakes as the inside ball hit the walls of the bell. The sound was like a sweet song from a long-forgotten memory.

The same wasn't true for the god. Phrixus clapped his hands over his ears and threw his head back. A terrible scream was torn from his lips as a dark portal appeared behind him. He stumbled into its inky mouth and slithery tendrils wrapped themselves around him. He clawed at their holds as he was dragged into the depths. The moment his outstretched fingers disappeared into the void the portal clapped shut with a bang.

With his disappearance, the End Time Winds vanished like ghosts at dawn. The sunlight rained down on us and melted away the portals. The water the funnels had stolen gently sank back across the lake. Spiros and Xander pulled our friends back into the muck as the waters lapped

MYTHS BEYOND DRAGONS

over us. I unmoored our boat from the bottom and we floated back up to the normal height of the water line.

Spiros looked down at Helle who he held in his arms. Her eyes were riveted to the spot where her brother had disappeared. Spiros gave her a small hug. "Will you be all right?"

She swallowed and looked up at him with a small, shaky smile. "So long as you're here."

I collapsed onto my knees and breathed a sigh of relief. "I am going to be sore in the morning."

CHAPTER 36

We sailed back to Psychi, an empty city with an empty port. Many of the longest docks were wrecked and their boards strewn about the length of the lake. We docked at one of the shorter ones and I gratefully stepped onto dry land.

That is, until I saw a familiar figure waiting for us on the shore. I was at the front with Xander when I froze midway down the dock. He, too, noticed the figure at the end of the planks and his eyes widened.

"What's the stop for?" Tillit shouted from the rear.

I shook my head. "It can't be."

But it was. There, standing at the end of the dock near a puddle, stood Kyma. She faced us and her soft blue eyes stared into mine. I continued onward and stopped at her side so I could stroke her soft muzzle.

Xander stopped on her other side and glanced over the horse at me. "Did we not leave her at Zem?"

MYTHS BEYOND DRAGONS

I nodded. "And in Tillit's stables. *Twice.*"

Darda furrowed her brow. "Zem? How did she travel there?"

I stepped in front of her and shook my head as I smiled into her bright eyes. "I don't know, but I really owe you one. You saved a lot of people back there, so-" I wrapped my arms around her neck and gave her a tight hug, "-thank you so much."

A bright blue light burst from her body and forced me to stumble back. Xander slipped behind me and caught me before I fell so that we both had front seats to the change. The long body of the horse shrank and grew in height to form the body of a tall woman of thirty. Long white hair as fluffy as the softest wool spread out behind her and a soft white dress covered her lithe form. Her feet were bare and her hands were clasped together in front of her.

The light faded and revealed her bright smile and blue eyes. She bowed her head to me. "Thank you, Miriam Estelwen. You are true to your name for you gave me hope as I had never had in these long centuries."

I blinked and raised a finger to point at her. "Who the heck are you?"

Helle gasped. "Lady Pani!"

"The lady fae of the lake?" Tillit spoke up.

She nodded. "Just the same, but my children and I were cursed by a jealous wizard and thrown upon the shores in the form in which you saw me."

"Your children?" I asked her.

She chuckled. "The pani are my children."

Tillit snorted. "That's a lot of kids."

"Yes, and their growing numbers were all that gave me the strength to continue in that horrible existence," she admitted.

"How did you come to be freed now?" Xander asked her.

Lady Pani returned her attention to me and opened her clutched hands. Nestled in her palms was a small, glowing round orb. It pulsed with a beautiful blue-green color.

I looked up at her smiling face. "What is it?"

"It is your Soul Stone."

My jaw dropped open, and I swear I heard the jaws of all my friends hit the planks. "My *what*?"

She chuckled. "Your Soul Stone, Miriam Estelwen. You granted me your power, and with it I have freed my children and myself from the terrible curse."

I clacked my jaw shut and shook my head. "There's no way I can do that! I'm only half fae!"

Xander looped his arm around my waist and smiled down at me. "I believe Crates told us you were now something more."

Lady Pani nodded. "Yes. You are a light against the darkness, and a comfort to those who need it the most. You are purification incarnate, Miriam Estelwen, and I hope to see you again some day. Thank you again, and I thank you for my children."

She walked through our group and down the dock. We watched her majestically walk away until a thundering stampede forced our attention inland. My friends and I looked back to the city and watched with gaping mouths as tens of thousands of little children, girls and boys but all with white hair and clothed in white, raced down the slope to the docks. They climbed the curved sea wall and, under so much weight and enthusiasm, the wall crumbled.

The children raced into the waters and dove beneath the surface, each of them leaving behind them a soft round fluff of wool. One of the children dove down near us. Spiros knelt by the dock and pulled up the bunch of wool. He turned to us and showed that a green stalk and roots connected the strange plant to the bottom of the lake.

MYTHS BEYOND DRAGONS

Tillit chuckled. "It looks like the pani owners are going to have to learn to sail."

The children disappeared, but the city was not empty for long. The citizens of Psychi followed them and learned from us the good news. There was much rejoicing among Xander's thankful people, but our exhausted bodies couldn't take the excitement, so we slipped to Tillit's house.

Upon entering a small figure streaked from the kitchen and attached herself to Helle's leg. Helle smiled down at her little bundle named Agatha. Agatha looked up at her with a frown. "You left me for a *long* time!"

Helle knelt before her and tapped her little nose. "Spiros and I had to save the city."

Agatha tilted her head to one side and studied Helle's face. "You look sad. Did something happen?"

Helle nodded. "Yes, but I'll be fine."

Mrs. Pachis emerged from the kitchen with a smile on her face and flour over her front. "You all look like you could use a nice, filling lunch."

"Put dinner with it, too, will you?" Tillit pleaded as he patted his stomach. "I'm starving."

She laughed and gave a nod. "As you wish, Tillit. Now all of you off to the dining room."

Spiros grasped Helle's hands in his own and raised her to her feet so they faced one another. "There is something I have meant to ask you-"

Helle smiled at his tense expression. "Will I go with you to your home?"

He nodded. "Yes, and of course Agatha can come and I swear I will-"

Helle reached up and pressed a finger to his lips. "Silly dragon. Of course we'll come with you. We'll always be with you."

Spiros leaned forward and caught her lips in a passionate kiss.

Agatha wrinkled her nose and stuck out her tongue. "That's disgusting."

Tillit nodded. "And appetite-suppressing, so if you two love-birds could handle yourselves for a few hours we can-ow!" He rubbed the back of his head and turned to glare at Darda.

She glared back at him. "Do not spoil the mood."

Xander stepped up to the pair and cleared his throat. They separated and Spiros looked up at his old friend as Xander puffed out his chest. "I have not given you permission to be wed, Captain Spiros."

Spiros drew Helle against him and grinned. "I fear a command cannot stop fate, My Lord."

A sly grin slipped onto Xander's lips. "I fear you are right, old friend. You have my congratulations, though I cannot say the same for the lady."

Helle blinked at him. "Why not?"

Xander winked at her. "Because you are getting the worst of the deal."

Our laughter followed us into the dining room where Mrs. Pachis had prepared a feast worthy of heroes. We supped like kings for an hour until a knock on the front door interrupted our merriment. We all stiffened as Mrs. Pachis strode out of sight to the front entrance.

The door creaked open and a male voice floated down the hall. "Is Lord Xander here?"

"Yes, may I ask who's calling?"

"I have a message for him from Captain Kokinos."

"This way, then."

In a moment Mrs. Pachis and a guard appeared in the doorway. The young man looked around our group. "Which is Lord Xander?"

Xander sat up. "That is I."

The guard bowed his head. "My Lord, we have received a letter from Zem."

MYTHS BEYOND DRAGONS

Xander arched an eyebrow and held out his hand. The guard strode forward and gave it to him. We all waited with baited breath as Xander opened the envelope and read the contents. A smile slipped onto his lips.

I winced. "What is it now?"

"It appears the dwarves and the people of Zem have agreed to do away with their differences and work together," he revealed.

Darda frowned. "And what about those horrible people?"

Xander chuckled as he tossed the letter onto the table. "Salome and Philip have been set aside in favor of the people." He looked up at the tense guard. "There is no need to worry, nor is a reply necessary. Enjoy the festivities."

The guard smiled and bowed his head. "Thank you, My Lord, I will." And with that he quickly departed.

I chewed on some delicious pie as I pondered the letter. "So they're going to try a democracy."

Xander arched an eyebrow. "That is a very appropriate title for such an experiment. Is there much of this 'democracy' in the other world?"

I nodded. "More or less."

"Let's have less politics and more eating," Tillit spoke up.

My friends dug back into the delicious food, but my thoughts wandered back to our ordeal. When night fell so did sleepiness, so Xander and I parted ways with our companions and went up to our room. He walked over to the dresser while I wandered to one of the windows and opened the glass. The bright stars twinkled above us like the gods winking at us.

I leaned my shoulder against the window frame and sighed. Strong arms wrapped around me, and I looked up into the curious face of Xander. "Is something the matter?" he asked me.

I shrugged. "I was just thinking about all the trouble just one god caused. He almost covered this whole place in those portals."

He nodded. "Yes. It was fortunate for us Helle chose our side."

I tilted my head to one side and furrowed my brow. "I. . .do you think-well, do you think the portals have a mind of their own?"

Xander arched an eyebrow. "That is an unusual question. What makes you ask it?"

I shrugged. "I'm not sure if it means anything, but they always took us to just where we needed to be. Kind of like they wanted to help us."

Xander pursed his lips. "I see what you mean, and present my own theory that perhaps the portals obey the whims of their users. We were sent where we needed to be because we wished to be there."

"So which theory is right?" I asked him.

He smiled and shook his head. "I doubt we will ever find the answer to that question."

I sighed and leaned my back against his strong chest. "You're no help. . ."

He chuckled and leaned down to peck a teasing kiss on my cheek. "And yet you still love me."

I rolled my eyes, but couldn't suppress a smile as I tilted my head back and looked into his grinning face. "You think we'll get a day off when we get back to Alexandria?"

He snuggled me close and looked out over the lake. "Who can say?"

The future could, but she wasn't talking.

A note from Mac

Thank you for purchasing my book! Your support means a lot to me, and I'm grateful to have the opportunity to entertain you with my stories.

If you'd like to continue reading the series, or wonder what else I might have up my writer's sleeve, feel free to check out my website at *macflynn.com*, or contact me at mac@macflynn.com.

* * *

Want to get an email when the next book is released? Sign up for the Wolf Den, the online newsletter with a bite, at *eepurl.com/tm-vn*!

Continue the adventure

Now that you've finished the book, feel free to check out my website at **macflynn.com** for the rest of the exciting series.

Here's also a little sneak-peek at the next book:

Forest of the Dragon:

> Cold. Cold and noisy.
> That was my world at that moment as I stood leaning against the railing of the large balcony. At my back was the imperial castle of Xander Alexandros, lord of Alexandria. In front of me lay the frozen surface of Lake Beriadan. Ice covered every inch of its waters, and children laughed and yelped as they slipped across its surface.
> Their voices were drowned out by the voices around me, and yet I was alone on the balcony. I grimaced and clapped my hands over my ears, but that did nothing to drown out the numerous voices. I threw my hands down to my sides and growled.
> "That is a rather intimidating noise," a voice spoke up behind me.
> I spun around and glared at the speaker. "Will you just shut-" I froze. Xander stood in the doorway that led into the castle. One of his eyebrows was arched. My shoulders drooped and I ran my hand through my hair. "Oh thank god, you're really there."

He frowned as he walked up to stand a foot before me. "Should I not be?"

I averted his curious gaze and shook my head. "No. I mean yes. Maybe?"

Xander cupped my chin in one hand and lifted my gaze to his. He smiled softly down at me and made my heart flutter. "What is the matter?"

I sighed. "Do you remember those voices I heard a few months ago? The ones Crates told us were the voices of the gods?" He nodded. "Well, I'm hearing them again."

He pursed his lips. "How long have they remained silent?"

I shrugged. "Ever since we defeated Phrixus two months ago."

"Are they the same as you heard before?" he wondered.

I winced. "That's the bad part. They sound louder. It's like there's a party in my head where I didn't invite any of them and they're all drunk."

"Can you understand what they are saying?" he asked me.

I drew my chin out of his grasp and wrapped my arms around myself as I shook my head. "Nope. It's just a bunch of murmurs, but I get the feeling from the tone of their voices that they think something's going to happen."

"Lord Xander!" On cue one of the castle sentries appeared in the doorway. He was low on breath, but still managed to stand at attention and salute his lord. "My Lord, a message has arrived from King Thorontur."

I furrowed my brow. "Who again?"

"The fae ruler of Viridi Silva, the forest to the northwest of my domain," Xander reminded me before he strode over to the guard. "What is the message?"

The guard shook his head. "The fae messenger would not-"

"Hey! Stop there!" came a shout from the hall behind the guard.

Xander strode into the passage with the guard and me close at his heels. We glanced down the left side of the hall and glimpsed a tall Arbor fae stride down the stone passage toward us. Behind him was an entourage of a half dozen castle guards who scampered after the dark-haired gentleman.

I glanced up at Xander. "I'm guessing it's Spiros's day off."

He nodded. "Unfortunately."

The young man stopped before Xander and bowed his head to the dragon lord. "It is a pleasure to see you again, Lord Xander."

The guards hurried up behind him and pointed their swords at the gentleman. The leader of the group glanced at Xander. "My Lord, he would not obey our orders-"

Xander smiled and waved his hand at the guard. "It is quite all right. You may return to your duties-" he glanced at the messenger, "-all of you. I will entertain our royal guest." The men bowed their heads and retreated.

I stepped up to Xander's side and squinted at the young man. He was about thirty with pointed ears and shimmering black hair. The man was as tall as Xander, but slim and with paler skin. His eyes were the greenish color of fresh moss on a tree trunk and his black hair fell down to his rear.

I pointed at him. "Don't we know you?"

"He is Durion, prince of the Arbor fae of Viridi Silva," Xander reminded me.

Durion smiled at me and bowed his head. "I have not forgotten your name, Maiden Miriam, nor the great deed you did for my people which can never be repaid."

I shook my head. "It's just Miriam, and don't mention it. It was more of a fluke than anything."

He lifted his gaze to mine and his eyes flashed with a brilliant green light. "I have heard of many other 'flukes' that have been attributed to your impressive powers as a Mare fae. Even to the ability to produce Soul Stones."

I shrugged. "More flukes."

"Prince Durion, please forgive me if I I sound rude, but what has brought you so urgently to my castle?" Xander spoke up.

Durion returned his attention to the dragon lord and pursed his lips. "Pardon my interest in your Maiden-"

I cleared my throat, "-that is, in Miriam's abilities, but unfortunately they may be needed. You see, the humans have returned to Viridi Silva, and even now nestle themselves once more in the ruins of their ancient city, Pimeys."

Xander arched an eyebrow. "When did this occur?"

"The large group of humans were noticed traveling through the forest some three weeks ago. They have taken up residency in the ruins of the formerly cursed castle and we have seen them repairing parts of the fortification."

"Have you made any attempts to contact them?" Xander asked him.

Durion nodded. "Yes. Several messages have been left, once by night beside the largest of the tents and another by arrow pinned to the castle walls. They have not responded, and after each attempt at contact more work has been performed on the defenses."

Xander pursed his lips. "What does the king make of these humans and their actions?"

"My father-that is, King Thorontur believes they mean to take advantage of our smaller numbers and reclaim their lost territory," Durion told us.

Xander studied the young fae. "I sense you do not share your father's belief."

The prince straightened and pursed his lips. "I have observed them a great deal and can find no signs of aggression."

"Even in their rebuilding of the wall?" Xander wondered.

He nodded. "Yes. I would do the same if I were making a new home of an old one, and there is the people themselves. The men have brought their wives and children with them."

"So you favor a diplomatic route with them?" Xander persisted.

Durion stiffened a little more. "I cannot say for sure, Lord Xander, but it is on that front that my father wishes to see you-" his eyes flickered to me, "-both of you."

I pointed at myself. "Why me?"

"That is a matter on which he wishes to speak personally with you," Durion revealed as he glanced at Xander. "Will you come?"

Xander bowed his head. "We will come."

I glanced up at Xander and pursed my lips. "You think we should? I mean-" I tapped my temple, "-there's the voices problem."

He nodded. "An ally has asked for my aid. I must not forsake him."

I sighed and shrugged. "All right. When do we leave?"

"Immediately."

Other series by Mac Flynn

Contemporary Romance
Being Me
Billionaire Seeking Bride
The Family Business
Loving Places
PALE Series
Trapped In Temptation

Demon Romance
Ensnare: The Librarian's Lover
Ensnare: The Passenger's Pleasure
Incubus Among Us
Lovers of Legend
Office Duties
Sensual Sweets
Unnatural Lover

Dragon Romance
Blood Dragon
Dragon Bound
Maiden to the Dragon

Ghost Romance
Phantom Touch

Vampire Romance
Blood Thief
Blood Treasure
Vampire Dead-tective
Vampire Soul

Urban Fantasy Romance
Death Touched

Werewolf Romance
Alpha Blood
Alpha Mated
Beast Billionaire
By My Light
Desired By the Wolf
Falling For A Wolf
Garden of the Wolf
Highland Moon
In the Loup
Luna Proxy
Marked By the Wolf
Moon Chosen
The Moon and the Stars
Moon Lovers
Oracle of Spirits
Scent of Scotland: Lord of Moray
Shadow of the Moon
Sweet & Sour
Wolf Lake

Manufactured by Amazon.ca
Bolton, ON